McRae's Last Trail

With the relentless bounty hunter Durell close behind, the badly wounded outlaw Maury McRae reaches the small town of Gray's Flat. Nursed back from the verge of death by the beautiful Heather Cordell, McRae discovers what life could have been. In need of money, his fast gun brings an offer of work from the ruthless rancher Max Nelson. Learning that his new job involves a serious threat to Heather and her brother is a dilemma for McRae.

Trapped in a hopeless set of circumstances, yet still hoping to begin a new life, McRae sees that dream fading away as a highly dangerous situation develops.

By the same author

Badge of Dishonour
Breakout at Salem Gaol
Canyon of Crooked Shadows
Danger in the Desert
Death Dances at Yuma
He Rode With Quantrill
Logan's Legacy
Midnight Lynching
Missouri Blood Trail
Railroad Rangers
San Carlos Horse Soldier
The Forgotten Man
The Hunting Man
The Long Journey
The Peaks of San Jacinto
The Protector
Broken Star

McRae's Last Trail

Terry Murphy

A Black Horse Western

ROBERT HALE · LONDON

ISBN 978-0-7090-8814-1

Robert Hale Limited
Clerkenwell House
Clerkenwell Green
London EC1R 0HT

www.halebooks.com

Nottinghamshire County Council Community Services	
Askews	
	£12.99

Typeset by
Derek Doyle & Associates, Shaw Heath
Printed and bound in Great Britain by
CPI Antony Rowe, Chippenham and Eastbourne

ONE

Reining his pony to a halt on the crest of Angels Hill, the rider looked down on Gray's Flat. It barely qualified as a town, being no more than a collection of low buildings straggling haphazardly across a level floor of baked earth. It was a picture of desolation rather than an attractive scene, but that meant nothing to him. All he sought was somewhere to rest up a while, somewhere to let his wound heal while he planned his future. With a high price on his head and a relentless bounty hunter on his trail, he accepted that there might well be no future for him to plan. Nevertheless, he had survived for thirty-three years against all odds, and wasn't about to resign himself to fate. The present crisis might well be his most serious ever, but there was hope as long as he had a six-shooter in its holster and a fast hand to draw it.

With a gentle jab of both heels, he sent the pony down the slope at a leisurely pace. The animal negotiated stones and cactus on tired legs as it struggled to keep to the trail, while the rider sat stiff and awkward in the saddle, reins in his left hand, his body twisted to favour his painful right side. There was a creek at the bottom, and his pony clattered down the last few yards of the slope to eagerly plunge its head deeply into the stream and drink with hurried, noisy draughts.

Allowing his pony to have its fill, he then rode closer to the town. He could see that its single street was crowded. There were irregular short bursts of gunfire interspersed by bursts of cheering that suggested some kind of celebration was in progress. Moving closer at the same steady pace, he pushed his Stetson back a little to lift the brim that had been shading his eyes. Through a heat haze he saw that it was some kind of shooting contest taking place, not a fiesta.

Not knowing what to expect in a strange town, his self-preservation instinct kicked in. He drew the pony to a halt. Resting his left hand on the high pommel of his saddle, he paused for a brief moment before grimacing with pain as he drew his Colt .45 from the holster tied to the thigh of his right leg. Holding the weapon at eye level, he spun the well-oiled cylinder. Satisfied, he reholstered the gun and moved carefully in the saddle, waiting for the agony caused by the movement involved in checking the handgun to subside. Then he moved his pony forwards over the short distance into the town.

With three saloons taking prominence over all other buildings, Gray's Flat was a town without pride. Ugly, devoid of greenness, it had been built with an absence of both planning and imagination. A treeless waste, it could boast of nothing but crabbed yucca, cactus, horned toads, scorpions, rattlesnakes and, the rider didn't doubt, iniquity.

Unnoticed in the excitement going on around him, he rode up to a hitching rail close to the rough board front of a saloon with a gaudy sign announcing it was the *Pleasure Palace*. Empty food cans, the majority damaged

6

and twisted, littered the street. Their labels removed, they glittered nakedly in the afternoon sun. There was a small supply of undamaged cans at the feet of an elderly, bearded man, while a powerfully built man in his thirties paced back and forth in the centre of the street as he addressed the crowd. His brutish face was made more unpleasant by an insolent grin as he looked around him.

'Folks, I put up a hundred dollars here today for anyone who can hit a can five times while it's in the air. A whole heap of you have tried, but not a man jack of you has plugged a can more'n twice, and most missed the danged thing altogether. Now I ain't deaf, and I've heard a lot of you muttering that it ain't possible. Now most of you knows me, an' knows that Reuben Nelson ain't no braggart.'

With that, the boaster fell silent. Drawing his six-shooter, he signalled to the elderly man, who threw a can high into the air. A hush fell on the crowd as the can rose, sparkling as it turned over and over. The audience was so enrapt that every man, woman and child gave an involuntary jump as the big man's gun exploded once. The can was thrown out of orbit by the bullet. Then four further shots followed in rapid succession. There was a concerted sigh of admiration as the battered can fell to earth. Everyone there seemed frozen into immobility.

Then a young cowboy close to where the can had fallen ran to pick it up and quickly examine it. Holding the torn and twisted tin can high, he cried out. 'Gosh-darn it, Reuben's done it! He's bored the can five times, just like he said he would.'

There was instant, thunderous applause. A man in the crowd shouted 'That sure was good shooting,' a sentiment that resulted in a chorus of loud cheering.

Holstering his smoking gun, Reuben Nelson arrogantly swung his gaze around the crowd. 'The hundred dollars is still there if anyone else wants to try. The offer still stands.'

A line from the Bible, learned during his boyhood education at a Catholic Mission in New Mexico, sneaked back into the mind of the newcomer: '*Vanity, vanity. All is vanity.*' Still in the saddle, he stared steadily and mockingly at the boasting gunman. Noticing that others were becoming aware of the rider's contemptuous glare, Reuben Nelson realized he was in danger of losing face.

Taking a few steps in the rider's direction, he raised his voice. 'Ain't no point in you sitting there passing silent judgement, stranger. Better for you to come down and earn yourself a hundred dollars by plugging a can five times.'

Unmoving, the rider weighed up the situation. The odds were against him. In his weakened condition it was possible that the effort of dismounting would cause him to collapse. Even if that didn't happen, the wound left by the rifle bullet that had carved a deep groove along his right ribs was sure to interfere with his aim. But empty pockets added to the difficulties in staying ahead of the killer on his trail. He was badly in need of money, and one hundred dollars would suit him nicely. Drawing in a deep breath to fortify himself, he slowly dismounted.

Welcoming yet more excitement, the crowd applauded him. Letting a wave of dizziness subside, he hitched his pony. Then moving gingerly to avoid putting stress on his injured side, he confined his walk to a stroll as he made his way to the centre of the street.

'I sure hope you're faster with a gun than you are at walking,' a grinning Reuben Nelson ridiculed his slowness. He added sarcastically, 'But in your own time, *compadre.*'

Ignoring this, the stranger felt blood trickling from under the makeshift bandage that he had tied around his chest. Knowing that to delay would defeat him, he nodded to the bearded man with the cans.

Unlike Reuben Nelson had, the newcomer left his gun holstered as the can soared up in the air. As the can reached its highest point, the stranger did a fast draw that had the scepticism of the watching crowd change to a concerted gasp of awe. Only dropping the initial foot of its descent, the can was halted by the impact of the first bullet tearing into it. Spinning away from the gunman, it was struck by a second bullet that had it pause, suspended in space. There was a cry of utter astonishment from the spectators as the can spun and shivered twice more. Still some ten feet from the ground, and driven twenty feet further from the stranger by his accurate shooting, the can was struck by yet another bullet. Then it plunged rapidly earthwards. But then the stranger fired again to send the can careening sideways. In what appeared to the watching crowd to be slow motion, the can at last hit the ground, totally shattered.

The same cowboy who had retrieved Reuben Nelson's can, ran to pick up what had been the stranger's target. Disbelief and excitement tightened his throat to make his first shout unintelligible. Then he gave the street audience the message. 'Six hits! By golly, six hits!'

A smattering of applause built to a crescendo. Holstering his gun, showing not the slightest self-regard where his amazing feat and the appreciation of the crowd were concerned, the stranger walked towards where he had left his pony. Weak and dizzy, his legs threatening to give out on him, he drew on every last vestige of his swiftly disappearing strength to keep himself on the move. No one watching could detect what that short walk had cost him.

A disgruntled Reuben Nelson walked up to stand staring at him, having McRae fear that the strongly built man was about to attack him. If that happened, then McRae knew that he would die there on the dirty, miserable streets of a God forsaken place called Gray's Flat.

Staring at McRae, Nelson obviously needed time to consider his next move. Then he muttered, 'You got lucky, stranger.'

Relieved to see Nelson walk away, McRae was leaning against his pony for support when a tall man, white-haired and distinguished, smilingly approached him. Dressed in expensive clothes, he was a hefty, big boned man, an aggressive, dominant type that takes the world by the throat and frightens success from it. His maturely handsome face had something voracious written on it. Though his wide smile was warm and friendly, his eyes were hard and cold.

'That was mighty impressive, stranger. Might I ask where you're headed?'

Studying the big man for a minute or so before answering, the rider then replied. 'That isn't a polite question to put to a man, mister.'

Momentarily robbed of his oversized self-assurance by the newcomer's unfriendly response, the older man recovered and agreed. 'You are right. I hope you can forgive me for asking.' The man extended his right hand. 'I'm Max Nelson, owner of the *Two Circles* ranch out in Cottonwood Valley.'

The introduction had been made in a sociable manner, and called for an affable reaction. But a deep-rooted need for anonymity had the newcomer hesitate. Then, reasoning that he wouldn't be known this far west, he took the proffered hand and introduced himself. 'Maury McRae.'

'Glad to meet you, McRae. I should explain that the maverick you just gave a gunplay lesson to is my son Reuben. He's gone off sulking now, but he'll get over it. Reuben and me purposely staged this little shindig here today, and you've won your hundred dollars fair and square.'

'Why give away a hundred dollars?' a puzzled McRae enquired.

'I'm hoping it will be an investment, not a gift, and I reckon as how you've proved me right,' Nelson replied. 'It's like this, McRae. We're having a heap of trouble with cattle thieves and suchlike out at the ranch, and we have a real need for a fast gun.'

'So that's what the contest was all about?' Understanding the situation stirred up interest in McRae.

'That about sums it up.'

'But why do you need me?' McRae questioned. 'Your boy proved himself to be just one bullet behind me.'

Dismissing this with a shake of his head, Nelson said. 'You are too modest, son. No disrespect to my boy, but Reuben isn't in your class. I've never seen a gun as fast as yours. Added to that, and this will make you regard me is a danged old fool, before his mother died she made me promise never to put our boy's life in danger. She never did adapt to the dangerous life out west.'

Reaching into his pocket, he drew out a fistful of double eagles and pressed them into McRae's hand. 'There's your prize money, son. And there's a job waiting for you out at the *Two Circles*. You can ride out with Reuben and me right now if you've a mind to.'

Unable to believe his luck, McRae reminded himself that he had to take stock of the situation. Right then he had doubts as to whether he would have the stamina to get back up in the saddle. An immediate long ride was out of the question. He needed time to recover. But the job was vital to him, and he used a lie in the hope of securing it.

'I'm grateful to you for the offer, Mr Nelson, and I'd be mighty proud to work for you. But I have a bit of business to attend to first, and I wouldn't be able to start work for a few days.'

'That's no trouble, son. Any time that suits you,' a pleased Nelson said. He gestured with his thumb towards the saloon behind him. 'But will you let me buy you a drink right now?'

McRae sought for a viable excuse to refuse the invite. He had difficulty in finding the potency to voice a reply. His wound was bleeding and aching intensely, while his legs threatened to give out on him. 'I really appreciate the offer, Mr Nelson, but I'm kinda in a hurry right now.'

'Then you be on your way, Maury,' Nelson said affably. Pointing to the west end of the street, he added. 'When you're ready to join as, just ride out thataways, and take the trail to where it forks a mile out of town. The left fork will bring you into Cottonwood Valley and direct to the *Two Circles* ranch.'

'I'll be there,' McRae promised.

He had struck lucky. His gun had been hired and the pay was sure to be good. All he needed right then was somewhere to rest up and attend to his wound. With a huge effort that left him breathless and his whole body soaked with sweat, he mounted up. He just managed to let go of the saddle pommel to wave a hand in farewell to Max Nelson, as he rode off painfully down the street at the same unhurried rate as when he had arrived in town.

Later that same day, in the town of Etheridge that was some thirty miles east of Gray's Flat, Miguel Morales strolled among the diners in his hotel's restaurant. Beaming a white-toothed smile, he lingered at the tables for a brief exchange of pleasantries. The personal touch was good for business. But then he hesitated, made nervous by the sight of a hawk-faced man with yellow hair, worn long, sitting alone at a corner table. Obviously straight off the trail, the loner didn't fit in with the hotel's regular, respectable clientele. Beyond all doubt, this was a hard man. At odd times there had been trouble at the hotel. Morales offered up a silent prayer that this wasn't to be one of those occasions. Knowing that the sheriff was out of town made it even more alarming.

Preferring to know right away rather than continue worrying, Morales forced himself onwards. Managing to maintain his smile as he approached the tough-looking man's table, he said an overfriendly, 'Good evening, *señor*. I trust that your meal is satisfactory.'

'An excellent repast, thank you.'

This answer had been given in cultured tones that astonished Morales. The yellow-haired man's polite manner was in total contrast to his rough appearance.

'Can I bring you another bottle of wine?' the immensely relieved hotel proprietor enquired. 'On the house, of course.'

'That is most kind of you, but I abstain from alcohol other than wine, and take that only in moderation. However, perhaps you might do me a favour?'

'I will do my best, *señor.*'

Placing his knife and fork on the table, the man paused for a moment before explaining. 'I called at the sheriff's office on arriving in town, but there was no one there. Do you happen to know the sheriff?'

'I do indeed, *señor,*' Morales replied. 'Sheriff Fernando Wood is a good friend of mine. In fact, he resides here at my hotel. I happen to know that he is out of town on business at the moment.'

'Do you know when he might return?'

'Tonight at the earliest, but most likely not until tomorrow I fear, *señor.* But he does have a deputy.'

'No, I must see the sheriff,' the man said with a shake of his head that caused his long hair to swing. 'I will wait.'

'I have comfortable rooms available here, and my rates are reasonable, *señor.*'

'I would like a room, please, and the cost does not concern me.'

'Then welcome to my humble premises, *señor,*' Morales said with a wide smile and a slight bow. 'Speak to my clerk at the desk in the hall. Now, I will leave you to finish your meal in peace.'

Walking off towards the kitchen, Morales found the door open and his chef standing in the doorway. He asked worriedly. 'Is there a problem, Carlos?'

'Not in my kitchen, Miguel,' Carlos responded. 'But the *hombre* you were talking to is big trouble.'

'Don't be fooled by his appearance, Carlos. He is a perfect gentleman.'

'It is not me who is fooled, Miguel. Don't you know who he is?'

'No,' Morales admitted anxiously.

'He is Durell, the bounty hunter,' Carlos explained.

14

'Cold-hearted killer is a better description, from what I know of him from when I was in Cheyenne.'

'*Madre de Dios!*' Morales exclaimed, fearfully. 'I have just offered him accommodation, Carlos.'

Carlos grinned at his employer's fright, and then shrugged. 'Durell as a guest ain't likely to be a problem. Having him on your trail is a very different matter.'

When taking his leave of Max Nelson, McRae had one problem with two options. Needing to recuperate, he could either get himself a room in Gray's Flat and risk the arrival of Durell, or take a steady ride to the *Two Circles* ranch, resting along the way to allow his wound to heal. Accustomed to a star-studded night sky for a ceiling, he had chosen the latter.

Leaving the small town, he had ridden his pony through an enchanted environment, a land of vast distances, warm sunshine, a brilliantly blue sky, and invigorating pure air. Faraway mountains had snow-capped peaks that protruded through haloes of cloud. It was the kind of territory that spoke silently of a mysterious past so far distant that it made the lifespan of man and his puerile difficulties ridiculously trivial.

As he had ridden through a cottonwood with the lowering sun throwing deep-orange shafts above the red buttes, he began to feel good. The pain in his right side had eased, and though the danger dogging his trail was still shadowing his mind, much of the power it held had faded as his physical condition had improved.

Riding through a wide clearing in the cottonwood, he had decided to make camp and allow the peaceful magic of the imminent night to embrace him. Putting his pony out to graze, he had lit a small fire and made coffee. Then he had laid out his bedroll and settled down. The fortunate events of the day ran pleasantly through his mind. The expert manhunter at his back would track him to Gray's Flat, but would then be baffled by the unexpected. Anticipating that McRae would keep moving, the bounty hunter would, with luck, bypass the *Two Circles* and keep riding. These consoling thoughts stilled McRae's mind, and he slept soundly.

Awakening slowly at sunup, he floated up to a shimmering surface of consciousness. All the physical improvements of the previous evening had deserted him. Desperately tired and weak, he heard birdsong greeting the new day. A beginning day that was no more than a blur to him, a mixture of dark and light shades. Hoping to clear his vision by closing his eyes, he found himself spiralling downwards into the unknown blackness from whence he had come. When he woke up to stay it was to find his sight restored. But he was as feeble as a hind-tit calf.

Gradually his fragmented thoughts came together. He had bled profusely during the night, and he could feel blood still pumping from his wound and running thickly down his right side. Taking advantage of a nearby rock, he managed to struggle up into a sitting position. Robbed of energy by the immense effort, sweat pouring from his brow, stinging his eyes, he propped himself against the rock to take a much-needed rest.

Head swimming, he was alarmed to feel himself sliding towards unconsciousness yet again. He pushed his body up into a kneeling position. In the past few hours he had lost a lot of blood. Sufficient to put his life in danger. Somehow finding a reserve of strength that though puny was sufficient to thrust him past inertia, he tore off his coat. His woollen shirt was saturated with blood. Unbuttoning it, he ripped off both sleeves and threw what remained of the shirt to one side, where it hung bloodily on a mesquite clump.

Knotting the cuffs of each of the sleeves together to make an improvised bandage that was both lengthy and wide, he caused himself agony by laying the material over the now gaping, bloody wound. Pausing to rest could well prove fatal. Awareness of this had McRae fight a debilitating nausea and rapidly increasing frailty, to wrap the joined shirtsleeves tightly round his chest and tie the ends. Reassured by the pressure on the wound, he put his coat back on.

Time was of the essence. No longer could he keep his injury concealed from Max Nelson. His only hope of survival was to reach the *Two Circles* ranch as quickly as possible, and ask for help. If that should mean he would be regarded as no longer fit for employment, then so be it. At least his life would be saved.

Even the slightest delay was out of the question. Staggering towards where his pony grazed contentedly beside a large, flat-topped rock, he fell to his knees twice before completing the short distance. Made skittish by the smell of blood, the pony shied away from him. Grabbing the animal's bridle to restrain it, McRae used the grip to swing himself up on to the rock, and from there into the saddle.

Inquiries that he had made when leaving Gray's Flat had him estimate that the *Two Circles* lay some ten miles up ahead. Slumped in the saddle for a few minutes, he then tentatively moved the pony out on to the trail. The going was as tough as he had anticipated, but he rode at an even pace, carefully avoiding the rough spots, though keeping as close to the trail as possible.

After covering a distance of about two miles, he learned that by letting his legs take the strain he could ease the agony that wracked his upper body. By pressing his feet hard into the ox-bow stirrups he could lift himself slightly from the saddle, thereby lessening the jolting of the pony's gait.

However, that relief lasted for only one further mile. Exhaustion sapped the power from his legs and sinking down on the hard, convulsing saddle had blood oozing steadily from his wound. Worse still, his mind began to wander. Everything around him seemed unreal. It was as if he had wandered into a land of dreams. His surroundings began to change instantly, and then just as suddenly switch back to what they should be.

At one stage he went back in time to Durango country when he had been sentenced to death for shooting a rancher's brother in a fair fight. He relived in harrowing detail how, by overpowering a deputy town marshal, he had escaped the noose with less than an hour to spare.

Snapping unexpectedly back to the present, he fumbled at his holstered gun as a five-foot-long rattlesnake slithered across the trail right in front of his pony. Any moment the sight of the diamond-back would cause his mount to panic, throwing him. If the fall didn't finish him, there was no way he would be able to muster the physical ability to get back up into the saddle.

But the pony plodded on unheeding. When McRae looked, the rattler had vanished as swiftly as it had appeared. 'I'm seeing things,' he thought aloud, and heard himself laughing uncontrollably. What he took to be the sound of insanity clicked his mind back into place.

A haze that affected him mentally and physically

replaced the madness. The reins slipped from his lifeless fingers and he grabbed at the pommel with both hands, clinging on with what little strength he had left. Unable to do anything other than let the pony plod on unguided, he swayed precariously in the saddle. Riding on with his head bowed, he tried to keep himself in touch with the world by watching the trail.

He may have slept, but couldn't be sure. Brought into something like half-consciousness by the sound of a whinny from his pony, he saw a shadow darkening the trail. He had a dim impression of a cabin immediately in front of him. Through a mist, he could make out the figure of a young woman sitting in a chair outside the cabin door. He heard her startled exclamation, saw her rise and run towards him. The expression on her face was a blending of concern and fear.

Incongruously, and in spite of his own condition, he was distressed by the realization that he was frightening her. Attempting to call out some kind of reassurance to her, his voice failed him.

The pony stopped. He slumped forwards, low over it's mane. From a distance he heard a man's voice say. 'Seems like I've come to the end of my last trail sooner that I expected, ma'am.'

It took a brief moment for him to recognize the voice as his own. Then from some much greater distance a female voice drifted through the air to reach him faintly. 'Oh, dear God,' it said. 'You are badly hurt.'

Leaning sideways, he half fell, half slithered out of the saddle. Luck had him land on his feet, but his legs felt rubbery, threatening to give out on him as he staggered towards the open door of the cabin to lean against the jamb, hanging on dizzily. Through a thick blackness he sensed the woman approach him, felt her hands on him, helping him into the chair in which she had been sitting. There was relief at being seated, but he was too far from consciousness to be aware of much else.

Then, faintly, he knew that she was laying him back in the chair and stretching him out full length. The pain in his side was excruciating now as she leaned over him. Striving to get up, he was pushed back firmly by her. He clenched his jaw defiantly as she used an instrument he was unable to identify in an attempt at getting his mouth open. Succeeding, she poured some kind of liquid down his throat. Gagging, he fought her, trying to knock away whatever it was she was using to pry his mouth open. But he was too feeble to resist.

'I have to stay alert,' he warned her urgently. Then the world rotated at a dizzying speed, hurtling him into oblivion.

TWO

The interior of the sheriff's office in Etheridge came as a shock to Durell. Its decor was in keeping with that of the classy hotel in which he had stayed the night. Pinewood walls, sanded and stained, were decorated with narrow-framed photographs, likenesses of the notorious lawless of the era clipped from WANTED handbills, a gallery of renegades in which all the faces were familiar to him. The ornamental desk was huge and uncluttered, on display rather than in use. In front of the desk with his hands behind him, grasping it to support himself in a half-sitting position was Sheriff Fernando Wood.

Dark-skinned, his lean, wide-shouldered body beautifully attired in a suit of dark material, the sheriff had a high-voltage personality that immediately affected Durell. He hadn't expected a sheriff this far west to be a well-dressed dandy.

There was no handshake. No social preliminaries. Though of gentlemanly appearance, the kind of man Durell would expect to keep such an unusual office, the sheriff was openly hostile. Even so, Durell wasn't fooled. For all his 'back East' dress and fancy surroundings, Fernando Wood was clearly a dangerously capable fighting man.

21

'I heard you were in town, Durell. What brings you here?' Wood said curtly.

'A desperado by the name of Maury McRae,' Durell replied.

'McRae has never been this far west.'

'He has now,' Durell informed the sheriff. 'All I am seeking is a likeness of McRae to show around while I'm hunting him. Plus your assurance that you'll allow me to do what I came to do without the kind of interference I've had from lawmen in the past.'

'Why should I make it easy for you to do what I'm paid to do?' Wood asked.

'Why not? The only difference between us is that you wear a tin star and I don't.'

'There's more to it than that, much more,' the sheriff disagreed, tapping the silver badge on his chest with a forefinger. 'This star earns me respect. Your chosen profession has you despised.'

'I take that to mean that I'm wasting my time asking for your cooperation.'

Pushing himself up from the desk, the sheriff walked round it to open a drawer and take out a stack of Wanted posters. Leafing through them, he pulled one out and studied it. Staring up at him was the picture of a strikingly handsome young man.

Wood remarked meaningfully to Durell, 'There's a mighty big reward on McRae. Enough to retire on.'

'There's a whole lot of counterfeit bad men around these days, Sheriff,' Durell said, 'but McRae is not one of them. To me it's a matter of prestige. I'm after the man, not the reward. When I meet him it will be face to face. I will be putting my own life on the line.'

Walking away, Durell had reached the door when the

22

sheriff called to him. 'Wait just one minute, Durell.'

Hand on the latch, Durell waited.

'Do what you have to do, do it quick, then get out of my territory.'

Lips parting as if he was about to respond, Durell gave no more than a curt nod before turning and going out of the door.

McRae attempted a rough estimate of how long he had been unconscious. The sun was close to setting, and the clearing at the front of the cabin had been invaded by lengthening shadows. That made it likely that four hours had elapsed. He was still partly sitting, partly lying in the chair outside of the cabin, the chair into which the womm had helped him on his arrival. That was now no more than a hazy memory for him. But recall of the agony and weakness he had suffered was still sharp in his mind.

He tried sitting upright. Anticipating a return of pain and nausea, he was pleasantly surprised to suffer no more than slight discomfort. He was wearing a shirt that was partly open, revealing neat bright-white bandaging round his chest. It was the work of an expert. That explained why he was feeling so well. He was studying the shirt, which was new and slightly too big for him, when a young woman came out of the cabin door to his right.

'It's my brother's shirt,' she answered his unspoken question as she placed a small canvas bag on the ground beside him. 'I'd better take a look to see how you are healing.'

She had to be the one who had come forward to meet him as he had ridden up to the cabin. She wore a blue-check gingham dress, the attire of a farmer's daughter off to enjoy the fun at a hoedown. But her face contradicted

23

this impression. Obviously an academic, her appearance was completely out of context with this wild environment. She had a wide, full-lipped mouth that didn't fit right with a slender but prominent nose. Strangely, the irregularity of features gave the girl a special kind of attractiveness such as McRae had never before witnessed in a woman.

'My pony?' he worriedly and weakly enquired.

With a faint smile at a Westerner's concern for his horse, she replied. 'Don't fret, your pony is fine. But you are badly hurt and we must prevent the wound from becoming infected. Even if it should not, there is still a very real chance of a fever.'

Mystified by her knowledge of such things and her medical skills, McRae tried to bring himself more upright as she started to remove his shirt. A sharp pain in his ribs and a disabling giddiness warned that his recovery was still at a very early stage. He slumped back, and she allowed him to rest for a few moments before slipping an arm round his shoulders to lift him a little so as to be able to remove his shirt.

Then she worked swiftly. Cleansing his wound, she smeared a yellow ointment on to a pad of gauze, which she then placed gently over the wound. It had an immediate and welcome soothing effect. Then she re-bandaged his chest and helped him back into the shirt. Exhausted, he lay back in the chair and closed his eyes, hearing her footsteps fading as she walked back inside the house. He didn't move for a long time, and when he did open his eyes he realized that he must have slept. It was night and a crescent moon was rising over a rim of far away hills. Feeling hot, he raised his left hand and passed it over his forehead. There was a film of sweat that warned him that he had at least a slight fever.

A dim light behind him and to his left had him turn his head. The yellow glow came from the cabin's window. He could see into the kitchen, where a kerosene lamp stood on a table. There was a stove and some kettles and pans hanging on the wall. The girl was in there alone, working at some task. Though she had mentioned a brother, McRae had seen no one but her.

As if sensing his gaze on her, she dusted flour off her hands and moved out of his view. He heard the rustle of her dress as she came out of the door and walked to his side.

'You are awake,' she said unnecessarily. 'Do you feel that you can eat anything?'

'Thank you, ma'am, but I don't think I could manage a thing right now.'

'That's understandable,' she said with a sympathetic smile, adding firmly, 'but you have something of a fever and can't stay out here all night. This is going to be difficult for you, but I will help you come inside. Let's get you to your feet.'

She was right. Even with her assistance the effort of getting up out of the chair made him feel terribly unwell. It was necessary to lean heavily on the girl, as she urged him to do, and he was amazed at the strength of her slight body. In the moonlight he could see the glint of determination in her eyes. Slowly and uncomfortably for both of them, they made it to the cabin door. Once inside, he was sure that he had neither the energy nor the resolve to take another step. Nevertheless, shamed by her fortitude and responding to her whispered words of encouragement, he managed to go through another door into a room containing a bed. Faint now, and threatened by unconsciousness, he staggered with her to the bed.

With what must have been her last ounce of strength, she turned him so that he flopped down on the bed on his back and lay still, hopelessly fighting a liquid blackness that was fast seeping into his mind.

He heard her voice, beside him and yet seemingly coming from afar. 'Try to remain awake while I fetch you some medicine.'

She went out, and it was a struggle for him to stay conscious. He was losing the battle when she returned after having been gone only a matter of minutes. Sitting on the edge of the bed she poured a spoonful of medicine from a bottle. Putting her other hand behind his head she lifted it a little to administer the liquid.

As she released his head and he lay back down, he heard her say. 'I will leave the medicine here beside the bed. Should you awake in the night and feel any distress, take one spoonful each time. If you need me I will be in the next room. So just call.'

Anxiously wanting to express his thanks, he found himself unable to utter a word. He thought that he heard the door close behind her as he tumbled into a pitch-black pit of unconsciousness.

He awoke several times during the night and each time shakily took a dose of the medicine. At what must have been well after midnight, he slept deeply without waking again until dawn. Watching the shifting patterns of shadows played on the walls by the rising sun, he lay quiet for a long time. There was a dull ache in his right side, but otherwise he felt strong and healthy. Even so, he was reluctant to believe that he could have made such a swift recovery. It was safer to accept that it was the promise that comes with each new day that had lifted his spirits. That way he wouldn't be disappointed later.

Hearing movement elsewhere in the cabin, and assuming that it was the girl, he decided to test himself. Carefully swinging his leg out on to the floor, he stayed sitting on the edge of the bed for a moment to let the waves of dizziness in his head subside. His boots were near the bed and he pulled them on. Buttoning up the borrowed shirt and tucking it into his trousers, he stood up. Delighted to discover that he could walk unaided, he went to the door and opened it.

Holding a coffee pot, she was standing near a table. Her eyes widened in astonishment as she saw him and exclaimed. 'Good heavens! It is a surprise and a great relief to see you looking so well.'

'It's all down to you, ma'am,' he said. 'If I hadn't met you I'd be a dead man this morning.'

'Please don't say things like that.'

'I reckon as how I was about to breathe my last when you took care of me. I'm real grateful, ma'am.'

Cheeks going pink with embarrassment, she avoided looking at him as she said, 'I've breakfast frying and the coffee is hot. You are welcome at the table, although it's a bright sunny morning and you may wish to sit outside. The air will do you good, but we don't want walking out there to tax your strength. It will be a while before you can get back in the saddle.'

Not having eaten for close to two days, the smell of frying bacon and eggs had him ravenous. The thought of sitting at the table with her had strong appeal, but he told himself that he needed to keep watch. She had removed his gunbelt when nursing him, and the relentless Durell could make an appearance at any time.

'I think you are right, ma'am,' he told her. 'The air will help things along. I've the chance of work at the *Two*

Circles, and I don't want to miss out.'

She went out of the door with him, not putting out a hand to offer help. But she studied him diligently to make sure that he suffered no strain. It was a novel and very strange experience for him to have someone fussing over his well-being. He had been a loner for so many years that he hadn't a clue that this kind of life existed.

She had an Eastern accent and a natural ease and poise that Western girls had not attained. Going back into the cabin, she left him to wash in a tin basin that stood on a bench off to one side. His ablutions over, he walked to sit in the chair and look out over a great stretch of flat country that was rimmed on three sides by a fringe of low hills. The sun had been up for some time. It was spreading its warm golden glow above the rim of faraway hills. It was reassuring that such a spread of open land meant that the bounty hunter wouldn't be able to sneak up on him undetected.

The aroma of cooking food had come out through the open door now, and he sat up in eager anticipation as he heard her footsteps. She wasn't carrying food. She held his rolled-up gunbelt with its holstered Colt .45 in both hands. Bending, she placed it on the floor beside him, and then walked away without uttering a word. Watching her go, McRae thought that though everything about her said she was from the East, her actions showed that she was versed in the ways of the West.

Feeling more confident with the weapon close to hand, he closed his eyes and was enjoying the warm caress of the morning sun when he realized she was at his side again. This time she had with her a plate of food and a mug of coffee on a tray.

'I could get used to this,' he told her with a smile.

'That's good,' she replied. 'It will be a while before you are fit to move on.'

Hungrily beginning his breakfast, McRae shook his head. 'I'm feeling real well now, ma'am. I'll be riding out either later today or in the morning. There's work waiting for me.'

'I strongly advise you to rest up for at least a week,' she warned. 'You have a serious wound, and you have lost a lot of blood.'

'I don't want to seem ungrateful after everything that you've done for me,' McRae began, 'but I've always been my own man.'

'That is very evident,' she said.

'Is that a criticism, ma'am?'

'On the contrary,' she assured him, blushing a little as studied him. 'Can I ask you something?'

When he nodded consent she continued. 'When you got here last night you said something about coming to the end of your last trail sooner that you expected. What did you mean by that?'

Put off balance by her perception and the concern on her face, he searched his mind for an evasive answer. He came up with, 'I was off my head at that time, ma'am, just rambling. Back along the trail I was going to shoot a snake that wasn't there.'

Her reaction signalled that though she may have accepted the bit about the snake, she didn't believe that he had been confused when he'd spoken of his last trail. Too polite to say so, she took the tray with the now empty plate and mug from him, and went silently into the cabin.

Returning some ten minutes later, dragging a rocking chair, she sat at the other side of the door to him, sighing deeply as she sat. Both of there were content to enjoy the beautiful day in silence. McRae discovered that he could take pleasure in her company without speaking. He sensed that she felt the same way, but feared that he was fooling himself.

They were so still that a deer approached, unaware of their presence. Noticing them suddenly, it broke the idyllic silence by fleeing through a patch of brush over to their right.

They exchanged smiles, and she said. 'We spoiled that poor creature's day.'

'I reckon so, ma'am,' he agreed, stirring in his chair, pleased to discover the movement caused no more than a tightening of the skin surrounding his wound. He enquired. 'Is the *Two Circles* far from here?'

There was something odd about her tone of voice as she answered. 'About five miles.'

'Do you know the *Two Circles* folk?' he asked.

'I know *of* them, but I don't *know* them.'

It seemed as if it was a taboo subject with her, and McRae was sorry that he'd brought it up. The tacit rapport they had enjoyed had evaporated. He strove to think of something to say to restore the harmony between them. He failed, and they were silent until she jumped to her feet.

'My brother is coming,' she exclaimed in a raised voice.

Already alerted by the sight of an approaching rider, McRae furtively lifted the hand that had sought and found his .45. The rider halted his pony. Sitting at ease in the saddle, he stared inquiringly at his sister and McRae. There was a holstered gun at his right hip, but McRae noticed that it wasn't tied down. He was the epitome of a cowpuncher, but McRae found it easy to convert that to the appearance of a steadfast homesteader. There was an atmosphere of self-sufficiency about him, an unstudied nonchalance that said he was ready to take care of anything this savage country might throw at him. The sister was definitely an Easterner, but the brother truly was a man of the West.

It was late in the evening when Sheriff Fernando Wood walked into the *Four Aces* saloon. He cursed under his breath at the sight of Durell leaning with both elbows on the bar. Though Wood was aware that the notorious bounty hunter would be interested only in the outlaw he was hunting down, the very nature of his chosen profession meant there was a very real possibility of trouble for others, especially lawmen.

That was something the sheriff didn't need right then. There was a serious situation escalating out at Max Nelson's *Two Circles* ranch that was likely to erupt disastrously at any time. His sympathy was with Nelson, who was having cattle rustled at a rate that no rancher, no matter how wealthy, could tolerate for long. In the criminal category of the West the rustler took a place beside the horse thief and the backshooter. But he was pretty sure that the rancher had an ulterior motive for putting the blame for the rustling on Zec Cordell and Ernie Roderick's *Double U* ranch. The railroads were pushing west into a new and untracked empire. The land boom was at its height, and he had heard a whisper that the railroad builders had already earmarked Cottonwood Valley.

A fortune awaited the ruthlessly ambitious Max Nelson if he took possession of the whole valley, if he used the rustling as an excuse to force the Cordells and the Rodericks off their properties. Wood knew that Max

Nelson had the power to make a devastating move against the Cordells and the *Double U* ranch. Always completely honest with himself, the sheriff was satisfied his budding relationship with Heather Cordell had no bearing on his determination to thwart Nelson in this respect.

Heading in Durell's direction, along the way exchanging polite greetings with local men and saloon girls alike, he saw that the bounty hunter was wearing two guns. There was a consensus of opinion in the West that two guns made for clumsiness, but Wood was sure there was nothing maladroit about Durell when it came to gunplay.

As Wood came up to stand beside him at the bar, Durell uttered a friendly invitation. 'Good evening, Sheriff. Will you do me the honour of joining me in a drink?'

'I'd prefer that you finish the drink you have and move on, Durell.'

'That's somewhat uncivil of you, Sheriff,' Durell complained. 'I have no intention of breaking the law in any way. The only reason I am kicking my heels in this delightful town is due to the fact that I creased McRae with my big fifty.'

'There's nothing heroic about shooting a man from a distance with a .50 calibre Sharps rifle, Durell.'

Signalling to the bartender, Durell waited while his glass was refilled and he had taken a long drink before he spoke again. 'I never miss from any distance, be it with a rifle or a handgun. That shooting was simply a ploy to slow him down, Sheriff. He will be holed up somewhere having his wound fixed right now. When he is fit again, I'll be there, waiting. Despite what you wish to believe, Sheriff, I'll face McRae fair and square. Having said that, I can understand your attitude toward me, Sheriff, for we are truly two of a kind.'

'I see no similarity between us.'

'Nonsense. We are both all too familiar with that strange exultation that comes with combat,' the eloquent Durell said, smiling thoughtfully. 'Every country in the world has the same natural system as us. They produce their bad men who, in time, are killed by their other bad men for the general good. From the moment I walked into your office, you and I have been sizing each other up, fascinated by the outcome should there be a showdown between us. Heraclitus was indeed right when he said at the dawn of thought in the Occident, that war is both father and king of all. You and me are warriors, Sheriff. It is strife and the thrill of the kill that feeds our lives.

'I don't agree. You are an educated man, who was surely destined for better things.'

'I have known *better* things, as you refer to them, Sheriff. I was a Congressman when Rutherford B. Hayes was President.'

Intrigued, Wood asked. 'What happened? I guess it's a long story.'

'Not at all, the answer is a brief one. I had what I can best describe as a revelation, and simply reverted to the ways of the Teutonic and Gothic forests. To my true nature.'

'A wasted life,' Wood remarked, shaking his head sadly.

'Not so, Sheriff. The only time a man is ever fully alive is when every breath he takes could be his last when facing an armed adversary.' Raising his glass, Durell continued. 'It's possible that I may be fooling myself, and there is another explanation for what you and I do for a living, a darker side to what is at issue. When I first came out West a wise old gunfighter told me that he killed his second man in the vain hope of getting the image of his first victim out of his mind. Maybe that old guy had it about right.'

Aware that there was a lot of truth in what Durell said, and not liking it, Wood argued. 'Could be that neither analysis of yours is correct.'

'Could be,' Durell replied with a shrug, 'but nothing will alter the fact that it is downhill all the way for the likes of you and me. Things are changing, Fernando. May I call you Fernando?'

'That would have it appear that some kind of relationship has been formed between us,' the sheriff coldly replied. 'I am Sheriff Wood to you.'

'As you wish, as you wish, Sheriff Wood,' Durell agreed in a slightly mocking way. He stifled a yawn, lazily plunged a hand into a coat pocket, produced tobacco and paper and rolled a cigarette. Lighting it, he puffed slowly and deeply, exhaling the smoke lingeringly through his nostrils. Then he continued. 'The days of the likes of you and me are numbered, Sheriff. Very soon the jungle they call civilization back East will replace life as we know it out here.'

Wood was saved from making a comment when young Pete Goodson, the straw boss for the *Double U*, came into the saloon and hurried towards him. 'Can I speak to you, Sheriff Wood, private like?'

Nodding assent, Wood gladly moved away from Durell. Full realization of the effect Durell was having on him hit him as he moved away. The strange blend of philosophy, high intelligence, and killer instinct in the bounty hunter made him disturbing company.

'Zec,' said the girl, walking to stand by her brother's pony.

'This man rode in last night, badly hurt. I've tended his wound, and he'll be moving on as soon as he's well enough.'

The brother dismounted, saying. 'You're welcome, stranger. I'll be with you when I've washed up.'

'No. I won't impose on you good folk further.' McRae got up from the chair, the feeling that he was intruding urging him to leave. 'I'd be obliged if you could fetch my pony.'

He was turning to the girl with the intention of expressing his thanks, when a wave of weakness hit him and he fell against the wall. She rushed to him, but her brother got there first.

'Help him back into the chair, Zec,' she ordered. 'He needs to rest for several days.'

When he had McRae seated again, Zec grinned at him. 'You'd better do as my sister says, mister. Heather studied medicine back East, and welcomes the chance to use her skills out here.'

'She sure saved my life,' McRae told him. He hadn't known her name until then.

'Heather is one very special woman,' the brother said proudly. Reaching for McRae's hand, he shook it. 'I'm Zec Cordell. You can stay with us for as long as you need.'

'I'm really grateful, Zec. My name's Maury,' McRae responded, habit making him reluctant to give his last name. But he forced himself to do so. 'Maury McRae.'

'Dinner will be ready soon,' Heather told him as she passed her brother a clean towel.

When Zec had finished at the tin washbasin, McRae was able to follow him inside, and the three of them sat at the table to enjoy a tasty if frugal meal. Evening shadows were beginning to darken the room as they ate, and Heather stood to light the small kerosene lamp that McRae had earlier seen through the window.

As she cleared the table, her brother suggested, 'It's real nice to sit outside this time of day, Maury.'

When they were outside and seated, Zec passed a sack of Bull Durham to McRae. 'Help yourself to the makings, *amigo*. Blame me if my sister gets all riled up about smoking being no good for you in your condition.'

They both rolled cigarettes and lit up. Inhaling deeply, McRae let relaxation seep through his whole system. It helped, as did the comforting smell of tobacco smoke in the air.

'I wouldn't enquire into your personal business, Maury,' Cordell began. 'But I would say that there ain't a lot of opportunity for a cowpoke seeking work around these parts.'

'I've got myself job at the *Two Circles*. I was on my way when I had to stop off here.'

A change came over Zec Cordell, just as it had his sister when McRae had mentioned the Nelson's ranch. Zec's lips tightened into a straight line and he spoke stiffly. 'I'm pleased that you have work to go to.'

THREE

'Seems to me that the way that Miss Cordell and you react to mention of the *Two Circles* means that Max Nelson isn't what you'd call a right good neighbour,' McRae observed.

'We have good reason for not seeing him that way. He has the power to make things difficult for the Rodericks and us. He's been doing that for some time now, and all the signs point to it being a whole lot worse in the near future. But that ain't no reflection on you, Maury. You working cattle on Nelson's spread don't mean we can't still be friends.'

Though McRae wanted to know more about the local situation, any chance of further conversation ended as a rider came out of the shadow of a nearby cottonwood. Even in the dusk McRae could tell that the newcomer bore no resemblance to Durell. The fact that Zec Cordell stayed relaxed told him that he knew the rider.

Young, tough and weather-beaten, a man of the great outdoors, he reined up in front of Cordell and McRae. As he dismounted he explained the reason for his visit. 'I was heading for home and thought I'd stop off along the way to look in on you, Zec. Maybe have us a smoke and a talk, like.'

'I'm right glad that you did, Pete,' Cordell responded cordially. 'Meet Maury McRae, Pete. This here is Pete Goodson, Maury. He's straw boss for Ernie Roderick out at the *Double U*. They don't come any better than Ernie.'

'Or Ellie, his daughter,' Goodson said teasingly with a sly grin at Cordell.

'If Pete's got a fault, it's trying to play matchmaker,' Cordell complained to McRae, who read much into the homesteader's boyish embarrassment. Zec Cordell was a good man.

Still in the saddle, Goodson was leaning forwards to study McRae intently in the dim light from the kerosene lamp. He suddenly and excitedly exclaimed. 'You're the guy from in town the other day! Gosh darn it, Zec. This guy's the fast gun who plugged a can six times; beat Reuben Nelson all to blazes. Old Max was quick to take him on at the *Two Circles*.'

This seemed to put Cordell a little off balance. Not commenting on what his friend had said, he enquired. 'You going to get off'n that pony of yours for a smoke?'

It seemed that recognizing McRae had altered Goodson's mind. 'Not tonight, Zec. Some other time.'

'That's a mighty quick change of mind, Pete,' Cordell remarked.

Without uttering another word, Goodson pulled his pony's head round, struck its flanks with the spurs and was gone into the shadows before either man on the porch could say one word. There was a short silence while the two men listened to the decreasing beat of his pony's hoofs. Then Cordell turned and spoke softly to McRae.

'I had you figured as a cowpuncher hired by the *Two Circles*, McRae. From what Pete Goodson says, seems as how Max Nelson has hired himself a gunfighter.'

Not understanding why this subtle change in the situation should affect Cordell's attitude toward him, McRae explained. 'It's not like that, Zec. Nelson's taking me on to deal with whoever is stealing his cattle.'

'That fact don't do nothing to ease my mind, Maury,' Zec admitted. 'It don't make any difference between us right now, Maury, and I pride myself on being a pretty good judge of men, and I guess that you working in that way for Nelson won't put us on different sides of the fence in the future. You are welcome to stay until you are fit to ride.'

A mystified McRae didn't know what to say, so he remained silent. He was both worried and intrigued by finding himself in a fraught situation between the brother and sister to whom he literally owed his life, and the rancher who had offered him employment for which he was grateful.

It was late on a morning one week later when McRae caught sight of the *Two Circles* ranch buildings that were spread over a considerable area of land. Leaving the Cordell homestead had been harder than he had expected. Though neither of them had made a conscious effort towards it, a close relationship had fast developed between Heather Cordell and him over the last couple of days. Their parting had been both silent and mutually unsettling.

When riding off, he had turned in the saddle to see her standing forlornly outside of the cabin. She had raised a languid arm just once, and he had waved a hand in return before riding on without looking back. Though he recognized that it had to be a final parting, he couldn't help hoping that it wouldn't be. Never having put down roots, McRae was bemused by his feelings.

The *Two Circles* ranch buildings were attractive, revealing evidence of regular maintenance. The ranch house boasted a sloped roof and paved galleries. Waiting at the door to greet him as he rode up was a smiling Max Nelson. The rancher eagerly ushered McRae inside and led him to an office, where he gestured for him to be seated.

'I'm later than intended,' McRae said by a way of apology. 'Things took longer than I anticipated.'

'We all have business of some kind or another to take care of, Maury. The main thing is that you got here.'

'I guess that your son won't be pleased to see me,' McRae suggested.

'As much as I hate admitting it, though he likes to play the big man, there's much of the child still in Reuben. But he'll be fine. Don't let him worry you.'

'He won't worry me,' McRae assured him quietly. 'But I won't work for two bosses. Is it accepted that I take orders only from you?'

Nelson agreed with a nod. 'I've given my son some responsibility in running the ranch, but you will deal direct with me.'

'Another thing is that I won't bunk with the rest of the hands.'

'No problem,' Nelson readily agreed. 'There's a room over the smithy that you can have.'

Rolling a cigarette, pleased to see there was no tremor in his hands, a guarantee that his recovery was complete, McRae lighted it and drew on the cigarette in silence. Then he asked, 'You said back in town that you needed a fast gun. Does that mean one or more of those causing you trouble are known gunfighters?'

'If that were true, would it worry you?'

'Not in the slightest, but a man needs to know what he's up against.'

'Of course,' Nelson said understandingly. 'Heading the rustling gang is Zec Cordell, a homesteader. His place is some five miles from here, set back off the trail. He's got guts, I'll give him that, but he's no great shakes with a handgun as far as I know. Ernie Roderick's punchers over at the *Double U* are just an average bunch of cowboys. Maybe one or two can draw quicker than a man can spit and holler howdy, but Roderick doesn't have anything that Reuben and the boys can't handle.'

Drawing hard on his cigarette, McRae blew a column of smoke up at the ceiling. He had been disabled by weakness and pain when he had last spoken to Nelson. Now he was his old, strong, forthright self. 'Then I don't rightly see why you need me.'

'There's two reasons, Maury. Talk of that sharp-shooting you did in Gray's Flat has spread far and wide. Your reputation can subjugate my enemies without you so much as reaching for your gun.'

Walking to the window, Nelson stood looking out. McRae spoke to his back. 'And your second reason for hiring me?'

It took the rancher a long time to answer. When he did so it was without turning to face McRae.

'The second reason is Sheriff Fernando Wood.'

'Where does a sheriff come into it? It's those stealing your cattle who are breaking the law, not you.'

McRae was worried. If he was about to hear an admission from Nelson that it was all a ploy to rob the Cordells of their land, then he couldn't work for the rancher even though he desperately needed money.

41

'For reasons of his own, that's not how Wood sees it,' Nelson replied with a sigh. 'If he should turn against me, there isn't anyone around here who could stand up to him, except you.'

'He's fast?'

'Faster than all get-out, Maury.'

'You are asking me to gun down a sheriff?'

'I don't believe it will come to that,' Nelson replied.

McRae gave Nelson a searchingly suspicious look. 'But you're telling me that you aren't sure that Cordell is stealing your cattle?'

'Oh no, I am sure,' Nelson said, pausing to bite off the end of a cigar and light it. 'I take the word of Sanchez for it.'

'Who is Sanchez?'

'My range boss, who also happens to be my stepson. He's been watching Zec Cordell and tells me that he hasn't the slightest doubt the homesteader is responsible for all the beef we've lost in the past nine months.'

'Then it's simple,' McRae commented, though aware that he could be talking himself out of a big-money job. 'Have your stepson pass the sheriff the evidence, and that'll be it.'

Holding his cigar high, Max Nelson studied it as if it were the most interesting object in the world. Then he answered evasively. 'It ain't that easy, Maury. His work as range boss gives Sanchez a full day, every day, and he doesn't have time to gather proof. Added to that is the fact Fernando Wood is as straight as they come, and I'll take a whole heap to convince him. Even so, maybe it's not true that every man has his price, but I've yet to meet a man who hasn't at least one weakness. The sheriff's flaw is his liking for Cordell's pretty sister.'

42

'Which is where I come in,' McRae guessed, suddenly despondent. He disliked hearing of the possibility of Heather being involved with the sheriff, or any other man.

'Exactly. What I want you to do first is get me evidence of Cordell's rustling to present to Wood. I'll be paying you a handsome sum to do that, and you won't even have to draw your gun. If you get the evidence and Sheriff Wood won't accept it, then you'll have to deal with him in the way of your choice. That will mean you'll leave Cottonwood Valley as a rich man.'

'Or stay right here in the valley forever as a dead man.' McRae responded mordantly.

'You are sure that is this man's name?' Sheriff Wood asked earnestly.

Across the table from him, Pete Goodson nervously used an index finger to circle the rim of the glass he held. 'Zec told me the guy's name before I'd recognized him as the fast gun.'

'And he's shacked up at Zec and Heather's place?' a worried Wood double-checked.

'He'll be staying with the Cordells till he's fit enough to move on to the Nelson ranch.'

It couldn't be worse! Fernando Wood groaned inwardly. Glancing across to where Durell was chatting with a local businessman increased his anxiety. The potentially explosive situation in Cottonwood Valley now had a fast gun and the bounty hunter pursuing him mixed in. Max Nelson was gaining the advantage, and gaining it fast. Heather Cordell and her brother would be the first victims if trouble erupted.

'Thank you for telling me this, Pete,' he said, adding awkwardly. 'Do you consider this McRae *hombre* is any

43

danger to Heather, or to Zec, of course?'

'I don't feel so, Sheriff. Maybe if the Nelsons set him against Zec, who knows? But when he was in Gray's Flat, and out at the Cordells' place, he seemed a right enough kind of guy.'

Hearing that brought at least a small amount of relief to Fernando Wood. Even so, an already volatile situation was becoming more complicated and precarious. He cursed the fact that McRae had chosen to remain in the area rather than riding on, with the relentless bounty hunter following him. That would have made life a lot easier.

'This here's Lennie Falk,' Max Nelson said as he and McRae stepped out onto the stoop of the ranch house. 'Laurie's the *Two Circles* roustabout. Most of the boys are out on the range right now, but Lennie will show you where you'll be bunking, then give you a run-down on the place.'

A mass of curly fair hair gave Falk a boyish appearance, but McRae put him somewhere in his mid-thirties. Giving McRae a friendly smile, Lennie did a quarter turn to signal that he was ready to take him on a guided tour of the ranch.

They went to the corral, where McRae unhitched his pony. Falk opened the gate to have it enter the corral, and then closed the gate behind it. McRae asked. 'Do you like working here, Lennie?'

'It's a good place,' Lennie answered with an enthusiastic nod. 'I been here since I was a youngster, and Mr Nelson's always treated me fair and square.'

As he finished talking, Falk's expression changed to one of sulky anger as he looked past McRae. Made curious by this, McRae turned his head to look behind him. A dark-skinned woman was coming from a garden behind the house. She had a figure that the thin material of a flax-coloured, calf-length dress showed off to best advantage. With her head held proudly high, the woman's carriage made her self-assurance evident. With waist-length black hair pulled back and tied with a red ribbon, she looked neither to the left nor the right as she walked to the door of the house and went in.

'Who is that?'

Falk's eyes were blank, but McRae's question flicked them back to awareness. There was discontent in his tone when he replied. 'That's the mistress. She weren't here when I came.'

'Sanchez's mother?' McRae speculated.

'Yeah, that's Juanita,' Falk said grumpily. 'I don't like either her or son. Come on, I'll take you round the place.'

Highly impressed by the ranch in general, McRae liked the unique touch of a picket fence that skirted the main buildings. A stronger fence ran around a sizeable area of good grass to form a pasture for horses. McRae had never seen anything like the large vegetable and flower garden at the rear of the ranch house. It had a neatness and layout that owed everything to a woman's touch.

Lennie Falk may not approve of her, but Max Nelson had obviously picked an industrious lady for a second wife. Chickens clucked and scratched around the yard, and there was a small herd of cows that showed signs of receiving extra care because they were milkers. Though Max Nelson was primitive enough to hire a gun to protect his stock, he was more ahead of his time than any other rancher McRae had ever come across.

An hour or so after McRae's arrival, the tranquillity of

the *Two Circles* ranch was shattered as the wagon outfit straggled in. They rode in singly or in twos and threes, suntanned, tough-looking, seasoned young men, clear-eyed and capable. They continued to stream in until there were thirty-two of them. Last to arrive was the chuck wagon and the remuda, then the ranch burst into life and frantic movement. Cowboys scrubbed the bunkhouse while others aired bedding in the obliging heat of sunlight.

Max Nelson came out to stand beside McRae. He wore a pleased smile of pride as he watched the return of his outfit. His wife stood at the open door of the ranch house, while his son Reuben, having ridden in earlier, was standing to one side. Although staying in the background, busy oiling his saddle leathers, Reuben was eyeing McRae menacingly.

Two men came riding up together and dismounted close to where McRae and Max Nelson stood. One was wearing a bowler hat in place of the usual Stetson. He had an admirable breadth of shoulder that testified to his strength. He was about forty-five years old. There were hard lines about his lipless slit of a mouth, a glint of insolence in his eyes, and an indefinable force seemed to radiate from him, impressing on McRae that here was a fighting man to be reckoned with.

His companion, who was younger and of Mexican appearance, stared with undisguised curiosity at McRae. He questioned Nelson. 'New man?'

'Yes, Sanchez, this is Maury McRae.'

Glancing at McRae's tied-down .45, Sanchez commented. 'He sure don't look like no cowpoke.'

'He isn't. I've taken him on to hunt down the rustling gang.'

46

With a long, sneering, dismissive look at McRae, the Mexican walked swaggeringly away.

Indicating Sanchez's companion with a jerk of his head, McRae asked. 'Who is the hard man, the *hombre* in the bowler hat?'

'Dean Razzo,' Nelson answered. 'Sanchez's right-hand man. I confess that he'd worry me if I didn't have him on side.'

'I've seen a few like him, and you sure would be right to worry,' McRae agreed.

It was the hottest time of the day when Sheriff Fernando Wood rode into the semi-deserted town of Gray's Flat. Desperately in need of a cooling drink, he was about to dismount outside the *Pleasure Palace* saloon when the sight of Heather Cordell further along the street had him change his mind. She was placing a basket of purchases on to a buckboard, and was about to climb daintily aboard.

Reining his pony round, Wood rode in her direction at a trot. Heather was leaning forward on the seat of her carriage reaching for the reins when the sheriff stopped his pony and dismounted. The ultrabright afternoon sun kissed her golden hair, setting it sparkling. Her skin was a delicate shell pink. As he approached he displayed a diffidence that was in total contrast to his normally poised and confident manner.

Removing his light-grey Stetson, he greeted her respectfully. 'Good afternoon, Miss Cordell.'

'Good afternoon, Sheriff,' she replied, amusement twinkling in her eyes. 'Miss Cordell? Why so formal, pray? A few weeks apart shouldn't cause awkwardness between close friends.'

Remaining quiet for a few moments, he made a

47

pretence at watching a cowpuncher water his pony across the street. When he eventually spoke it was without raising his eyes to her. 'I guess I'm being mighty silly, Heather. Like some kinda shy kid.'

'In a land filled with brash, noisy men, that is a quality that I quite admire, Fernando,' she complimented him. 'What brings you to our fair town?'

'I thought it time I paid what I see as a peacekeeping visit to the *Two Circles*.'

'Stopping off at our place along the way, I trust, Fernando?'

With a nod and a sheepish smile, Wood said, 'I was hoping to, Heather. I understand that you have a guest.'

'We cared for an injured man, Fernando, but he left this morning.'

'I see. I would like to have a chat with you and your brother.'

'You've never needed an invitation from either Zec or from me,' she chided him. 'Why not ride back with me now?'

'I'd like that mighty fine,' he agreed.

Putting his hat back on and tying his pony to the rear of the buckboard, he climbed up onto the buckboard seat beside her.

McRae had ridden away from the *Two Circles* ranch through the afternoon sunshine. Having learned the lay of the land from Max Nelson, he now came out of a little gully and rode along the crest of a ridge that rose above endless miles of plains. Riding down a long slope, he struck the level and moved his pony at a slow lope through a shallow washout.

For a while he moved along at a brisk pace, then reined

up to breathe his pony. Lifting one leg up over the pommel he did a quarter turn in the saddle to sweep the plains with a probing stare. High up in the shimmering white of the desert sky a Mexican eagle swam on slow wings, shaping its meandering course toward the timber cluster that fringed a rocky stretch. McRae moved his pony at a walk over rock-hard ground toward the spot that the large bird was hovering over.

The terrain suddenly softened under the pony's hoofs. Looking down, McRae's interest quickened as he saw the tracks left by a herd of cattle. Dismounting, he sat on his heels for a more detailed study. Set a little apart from the cattle trail was the hoofprints of three mounted horses. According to Max Nelson, no *Two Circles* beef should have been in this area over the past year or so.

At the side of the tracks he found what had interested the hovering bird. A dead cow lay close to an overhanging rock rim. The left foreleg of the creature was broken, with the bone protruding jaggedly through the skin. A bullet hole in the cow's forehead told the story eloquently. The cow had fallen and he guessed it was rustlers who had put it out of its misery.

Just one question remained. He untied his bandanna and held it over his nose and mouth to filter the fetid stench of the decaying flesh. Leaning over the carcase he saw the proof that he needed. The cow had a brand of two overlapping circles. Straightening up with a sigh of satisfaction, he thanked luck and a circling bird for bringing him evidence of rustling so rapidly and easily.

With a wave of gratitude to the still-hovering Mexican eagle, he mounted up and was on his way once more. Aware that he must be nearing Zec and Heather Cordell's homestead, he left the cattle trail and urged his pony up an incline to a plateau studded with fir balsam and pine.

From the edge of the plateau dropped a wide, yellowish-brown valley, luxuriant with bunch grass, a suntanned sweep that nestled between some hills. Raising a hand to shade his eyes, he could see the Cordell homestead in the far distance.

Already the evidence seemed stacked against Zec Cordell as McRae rode down the slope to once again pick up the trail of the rustled herd. The trail curved slightly, leaving the homestead on its left. But one of the three drovers had gone off at a tangent, heading directly for the Cordell settlement.

Less than a mile further on, he saw the tracks where the rider who had turned off a way back had returned to join the other two drovers. McRae was devastated. It had to be Zec Cordell, who had ridden home to see his sister before coming back to help drive the rustled herd to his friends at the *Double U* ranch.

It was all the evidence necessary, but he was uncertain as to whether or not to let Max Nelson know of his discovery. He turned to ride back to the *Two Circles* ranch, hoping to reach a decision along the way.

'So, this McRae *hombre* is a desperado?' Zec Connell, a loaded fork raised, stopped eating to ask.

Across the table from him Sheriff Wood give a confirming nod. 'A dangerous man made desperate by being hunted down.'

'Honestly, I find that difficult to believe,' an unhappy Heather said softly. 'He was quiet in manner, unobtrusive. He was taciturn, I admit, yet also polite.'

'In my experience, Heather, the most dangerous of men are apt to be quiet and smooth-spoken. I think you will find many of his victims between here and New Mexico ready to disagree with you,' Wood advised.

'My sister always sees the best in even the worst kind of people,' Zec said with a fond smile at Heather. 'With McRae now working for Max Nelson, what do we hope for, Fernando, that the bounty hunter will get him before he can get to us?'

'That isn't likely, Zec. Durell is a perfectionist and more of a showman than Bill Cody ever was. He'll wait until he can call McRae out in Gray's Flat when there's plenty of people on the street.'

'So anything could happen while we're waiting.'

Wood wondered if this was the time to alert his friends to the possibility that Nelson's plan was to take over the whole valley to get a good price if the railroad did head this way. He decided against it, as he didn't want to worry them with something that may never happen. Instead he cautioned them, 'If Nelson can produce evidence, fabricated or otherwise, he'll doubtless use McRae to make a move on you.'

'I don't think so,' Heather protested. 'I can't imagine him doing Max Nelson's dirty work. We showed him kindness, hospitality. He didn't strike me as a man who would forget that.'

Shaking his head, a worried Zec told her, 'Anything's possible with an outlaw, Heather. What do you advise, Fernando?'

'I can't say until we see how things shape up. I'll spend as much time as I can here in the valley.'

'But you have a huge territory to cover,' a despondent Heather pointed out.

'I'll be staying close to home,' Zec Cordell promised. 'I'll not only take care of Heather, but I've got a duty toward Ernie Roderick and his wife in this. Me and their Ellie have been talking of getting married, and Max Nelson's saying that Ernie's helping me in rustling his beef.'

The sheriff looked sternly across the table at Zec, 'I wouldn't advise that you face McRae.'

'You're saying that I should turn tail and run?'

'I know better than to make such a suggestion to a man like you. But McRae is a fast gun, Zec, a really fast gun.'

Though she hadn't finished her meal, Heather stood, her worried gaze switching between her brother and the sheriff. Then, without saying a word she turned and walked slowly out of the room, her shoulders slumped.

FOUR

It was late evening when McRae neared the *Two Circles* ranch. He had travelled slowly over the last mile or two, held in awe by the glorious sunset. The sky in the west was afire with colour, deep red and gold and violet; a veil of subtle rose and amethyst enveloped the mountains in a misty haze. Purple beams darted from distant canyons to fuse with the radiant colours, glowing, shimmering, ever changing.

Although enthralled by the beauty, it was a sight that brought home to him the hopelessness of his present situation. The result was an immense sadness. Even more keenly did he feel the grim lonesomeness that had been his unwelcome companion since leaving Heather Cordell. The mystery that was night had awakened to fill the world, reminding him of how good life could have been. How it could now never be for him.

The moon rose, a pale yellow disc above the hills that rimmed the valley. Dismounting, he climbed a bald rock spire. In the western and southern distances were the plains, silent, vast, unending. Now below the horizon, the sun's remaining red light was slowly turning into saffron and violet as it blended with the shadows below the hills.

At that instant his self-preservation instinct sent an urgent warning through his body as he became aware of someone or something behind him. He turned sharply in his tracks, his right hand falling swiftly to his holstered gun. Not over six yards distant stood a pony and rider, both no more than a single silhouette in the gathering shadows.

'Don't shoot.'

It was a female voice with a bubble of amusement in it. Dismounting, the rider climbed towards where McRae stood. She moved lightly, as soundless as a mountain lion. As she came closer she pushed her sombrero back from her forehead. He was stunned to recognize Juanita Nelson. She was dressed in a riding skirt, dainty boots, gauntleted gloves, and a blue blouse of shiny material. The subtle shades of twilight emphasized her prominent cheekbones and the firm line of her jaw. It was a face that had a mature, unselfconscious kind of attractiveness.

'Have you ever seen such magnificent colours?' she asked wonderingly as if they were friends who had arranged to meet here. Her face was spellbound with sheer enchantment. 'This is my favourite place. I come up here often at this time of the day.'

'It's real nice, ma'am,' McRae concurred, made uneasy by being out in the night with the wife of his boss. He did a quarter turn. 'I'm heading back to the ranch. I've had a long day.'

Placing a gloved hand on his arm, she stayed him. She spoke quietly, matter-of-factly. 'Wait just a short while. It will be in your own interest to hear what I have to say.'

'What could you possibly have to say that would interest me?' a puzzled McRae queried. 'We are total strangers.'

Yet, intrigued by the earnest expression on her dark-skinned face, he turned to face her.

'How long might you be staying, sir?'

Martha Tinkler, the middle-aged proprietor of the small building that passed for a hotel in Gray's Flat, politely enquired of her visitor. Normally calm and reserved, she was more than a little flustered. In the dull glow of an oil lamp, she had initially been alarmed by her potential guest's wild, longhaired appearance, but she was now thrilled by the sophistication so evident in his manner and conversation. Accustomed to having unrefined ranchers and loud-mouthed, often drunken, drummers stay at her establishment, she awaited an answer hopefully.

'It could well be some considerable time, madam,' the man replied.

'Miss,' she corrected him blushingly. 'Miss Tinkler.'

'My apologies, Miss Tinkler,' he responded with a disarming smile. 'I really like the look of Gray's Flat.'

'You're welcome to stay at my establishment for as long as you wish, Mr' – she glanced down at his signature on the register – 'Durell. May I enquire what line of business you are in?'

'Of course you may. My interest lies in matters concerning the law.'

'Then I believe that you will be welcomed unreservedly, Mr Durell,' she exclaimed delightedly. 'Our little town needs a lawyer to enable it to grow in a civilized manner the way we wish it to. I am a member of a small group of citizens that is preparing the way for the formation of a town council. Should you require any information, don't hesitate to ask.'

'Most kind of you. I probably will have a need of some

local knowledge. I imagine that this far west you rarely encounter renegades, outlaws, that is?'

'If only you had been here yesterday, you could have obtained a *bona fide* answer to that question,' Miss Tinkler said, a sigh supporting her tone of regret. 'Sheriff Fernando Wood was in town.'

'Oh dear. What a shame. I take it the sheriff has since left?'

'I'm afraid so. But I don't believe he will have gone far, Mr Durell.' Martha Tinkler was desperate to prolong the conversation. 'I saw him leave with Miss Cordell.'

'Miss Cordell?'

'Yes, young Heather. She and her brother have a homestead not far out of town.'

'Maybe I'll catch the sheriff on his way back,' Durell supposed. 'I am most obliged to you for your courteous and helpful welcome to Gray's Flat, madam.'

'My pleasure, Mr Durell. Now, let me show you to your room.'

'In a way, we are not really strangers, McRae,' Juanita Nelson said, her lips struggling with a tentative smile.

Then the smile took hold and moved up to include her dark eyes. 'I'm blessed, or possibly it is cursed, by having a phenomenal memory. I spent some time in the Durango country before coming here, where I met and married Max Nelson. You were regarded as an infamous desperado there, but I admired you from afar, so to speak. I came to know you through your reputation. I was there when you had a showdown with Sol Clayton. They said he was the best, but you proved them wrong. I never before witnessed such iron nerve in a man, or saw such brilliant, blindingly fast gunplay.'

'There's nothing to be proud of in killing a man.'

'Nevertheless,' she said breathlessly. 'You have lived life to the full, and I envy you.'

'There isn't much to be envied in my kind of life, Mrs Nelson.'

'I disagree,' she said with a shake of her head. 'My husband is an intelligently selfish man, who has a moronic bully for a son. My own son, Sanchez, has grown to be exactly like his father, a man I came to regard with an intense hatred.'

McRae realized that this was no chance meeting. 'You came out purposely to see me?'

'Yes. I saw in which direction you rode out earlier, and guessed you would be returning the same way. I wanted to warn you.'

'About what?'

'About the situation here at the ranch,' she replied.

'It is not of any real interest to me, Mrs Nelson. Your husband hired me to deal with a gang of rustlers, and I'm happy to do so.'

'If only it were that simple,' she sighed, looking past him into the night. 'Please believe me. You are being used in a vicious scheme that will cause suffering for other people in this valley.'

This had McRae worried about Heather and Zec Cordell. 'How could that happen, ma'am?'

'I have said too much already,' she said, frowning. 'You should ride away now, tonight.'

'I can't do that. I need money.'

Accepting this with a nod, she advised. 'Then study what is going on here. Don't be fooled by Max Nelson. He is a devious person, and would have told you nothing of his plans. He is a land-pirate, McRae.'

'He's simply hired me to deal with the gang stealing his cattle.'

She nodded. 'On the face of it, that is so, but maybe you are being drawn into a scheme that will place you between Sheriff Wood and Max Nelson. That would be a mighty dangerous position to be in, McRae.'

'I am grateful to you for warning me, Mrs Nelson,' McRae said. He needed time alone to ponder on what lay behind the half-message she had given him.

'There's no need to thank me. The only pleasure I get these days comes from being disloyal to my husband. How bad does that sound?'

'It's not for me to say, ma'am. I guess that you have good reason to feel that way.'

'Oh, I have good reason. Believe me, I have good reason, McRae.' Without another word, she turned and walked away from him. He watched as she placed a slender, booted foot into the ox-bow stirrup, and swung gracefully up into the saddle and moved off into the thickening shadows of night until both she and her horse vanished into the darkness.

Though most of the magic in the night scene had faded for McRae, he lingered for a while so as to allow Juanita to arrive at the ranch long before he did. Eventually mounting up, he rode slowly, deep in thought. What the Mexican woman had said, though inconclusive, reinforced his suspicion that things at the *Two Circles* weren't what they seemed to be.

All was quiet in the night as he and his pony approached the corral gate at walking pace. Dismounting, he undid the cinch and removed the saddle in preparation for putting his pony into the corral. The sound of the bunkhouse door slamming like an explosion in the night alerted him to the possibility of trouble. He paused, waiting, but there was no new sound. Yet the silence that had fallen on the night was pregnant with a premonition of danger.

About to lift his saddle from the corral rail, a slight noise behind him had him spin round. The sight of the huge figure of Reuben Nelson looking out of the darkness had him release the saddle. Not knowing exactly what to expect, but aware that whatever it was would prove hazardous, he waited. The evidence of the rustling of *Two Circles* stock, though it could only be described as scant at that time, more than suggested that Reuben Nelson and Sanchez were involved, and had good reason to not want him around.

'Put that saddle back on your horse, McRae. Then mount up and ride out, and keep on riding,' Nelson ordered menacingly. 'There's no place for you here.'

Though the moonlight was weak, McRae could see that Nelson wasn't wearing a gunbelt. That meant that in confronting him the big man wasn't going to risk gunplay, but would rely on the power of his massive, muscle-packed body.

'I'm not figuring on going anywhere, Nelson,' McRae replied in a low, conversational tone. 'Your father hired me, and he sure hasn't said anything about firing me.'

'I'm firing you, right now, McRae.'

'I don't think so.'

In a deliberate ploy to invite an attack, McRae turned his back on Nelson as if to reach for his saddle. The tactic worked. As Nelson lunged a him, McRae turned on his heel, took a short sidestep, then delivered a blow to the body with his left hand. As he had guessed, though the rest of Nelson's body was solid muscle, his over-large stomach was soft. McRae's fist sank in deep, bringing a gasping grunt from the rancher's son.

Following up rapidly on this temporarily disabling punch to the midriff, McRae released a hard right-hand blow to the side of Nelson's face, which was in profile to him. Sagging at the knees, the big man staggered sideways away from McRae, who went after him, mercilessly ripping in punches to the body and head. Driven backwards by the battering, Nelson's back came up against the corral, trapping him.

Bleeding with a bubbling rattle from the nose and mouth, in agony from the body punching, the rancher's son was barely conscious. In desperation, he swung a wild right hand that caught McRae on the side of the neck, sending him toppling sideways to collide with his pony. Panicking, the animal reared, knocking McRae off his feet.

Hurtling through the air, hitting the ground hard, face down, McRae struggled to stem the wave of blackness swelling through his head. Succeeding, he was coming up on his hands and knees, getting ready to resume the hammering he had been giving Nelson.

But there was no time to get to his feet, no chance to recommence his attack, no possibility of defending himself. Face distorted by rage, his opponent had had time to recover sufficiently to push himself away from the corral fence and stagger over to deliver a vicious kick to McRae's ribs.

Pain knifed through the whole of McRae's body as he was aware of the wound in his side bursting open and blood erupting thickly. Hot and sticky, it was a grim reminder of what he had recently suffered from the injury caused by the large bullet from a rifle that had ploughed a deep channel through his flesh.

Collapsing, he saw Reuben Nelson's leg raised and his heavy boot coming towards him again. Stealing himself to withstand yet more extreme agony, he was saved from that torture as he blacked out.

'I have good news, Juanita, really good news,' a pleased Max Nelson announced as he poured a drink and walked to place it on the small table where his wife sat.

Taking the glass, a bored Juanita sipped the drink while she waited for her husband to continue. It was difficult to concentrate, as most of herself seemed to have remained with McRae out in the wild and brilliantly colourful display by nature that they had shared.

'A messenger rode in earlier this evening. In two days time I'll be going into Etheridge,' Max Nelson went on. 'A meeting has been arranged between the railroad executives and me. It's certain now, Juanita. The railroad will be coming through Cottonwood Valley. We are wealthy people now, but we'll have riches beyond belief when I have clinched this deal.'

Though desperately needing to enquire about the Rodericks and the Cordells, who shared the valley with them, Juanita remained silent. Her husband would have a scheme to deal with them that would be as foolproof as his projected meeting with the railroad people.

Concern for their neighbours had her break her silence to ask hesitantly, 'What of the others who have settled in the valley?'

'The others?' he snorted. 'Had they not been robbing me blind, Juanita, I'd make sure they get a fair deal. As it is, they will be getting exactly what they deserve.'

A shudder ran through her as she heard this. Now she

fully understood why Max Nelson had hired a fast gun like Maury McRae. She doubted that McRae knew yet why he was here at the *Two Circles* ranch. She wondered how he would react on discovering the real reason Nelson had employed him. It was getting late and she was tired. Too tired to listen to her husband's lust for money and power. Too weary to fret over the fate of the innocent people in the valley who were soon to suffer.

Emptying her glass, she stood and was about to walk out of the room, when there was an urgent banging on the front door of the house. Alarmed, she followed her husband as he hurried to open the door. Standing on the stoop was Lennie Falk and another cowhand, supporting between them an ashen-faced Maury McRae. Juanita released an involuntary cry of horror as in the lamplight from the hall she saw that McRae's shirt was sodden with blood.

'Take him into the spare bedroom on the right,' Max Nelson ordered the two men. 'Then you, Lennie, ride into Gray's Flat and bring Doc Faylen out here, pronto.'

Having watched the rider come out of the rising sun, Heather Cordell's anxiety increased as he approached the cabin unhurriedly. Zec had left soon after dawn to help with branding at the Rodericks' ranch, and there was something about the stranger heading her way that had her fervently wishing that her brother had stayed at home that day.

As he came closer she saw that the horseman had the appearance of an imitation desperado. One of an increasing new breed of pretend bad men from the East who were despised by true Westerners. His yellow hair was shoulder length, and he wore ultra-Western clothing.

62

Alarmed, she stepped quickly into the cabin and reappeared, holding the scattergun that was kept always behind the door. She stood rigid on the porch, her eyes blazing defiance though her heart was racing.

But as he reined up his horse in front of her, the stranger's harsh and frightening features were transformed by a genuinely pleasant smile.

'Good morning, miss,' he said in sophisticated tones such as Heather hadn't heard since moving out West to join her brother. 'Please believe that you have no cause for alarm.'

She admitted to herself that she had been wrong. There was nothing counterfeit, no cheap pretentiousness about this man. Feeling foolish, she first lowered the scattergun, then propped it against the cabin wall and left it there.

'Do you wish to water your horse?' she asked.

The stranger looked around the homestead, taking a mental inventory that included just her pony in the small corral, a sure sign that she was alone. That troubled Heather.

He replied. 'That is kind of you, ma'am, but I've only had a steady ride out from Gray's Flat. I'm thinking of settling in town, so I'm enjoying myself by taking a look at the surrounding countryside. This is a fine place you have here.'

'It suits my brother and I,' she said, pointedly adding. 'He is due back home at any moment.'

'I would like to meet him,' the stranger said. 'Did he develop this place from scratch?'

'Yes. It was no more than a wilderness when Zec purchased the land.'

'He's made a praiseworthy job of it,' he commented,

63

taking another look around. Then, with a concerned frown, he asked a totally unexpected question. 'I hope that your brother is not injured or anything like that, miss?'

Despite the heat, a sudden shiver ran through her. In a voice that had a tremor in it, she enquired, 'Why do you ask such a thing?'

'I apologize, miss. That was an insensitive question to ask, and I much regret causing you alarm. It's just that I came across some bloodstained clothing a little way back along the trail.'

Then realization dawned on Heather. Though phrased casually, it was the query of a manhunter that revealed who her visitor was. This was Durell, the bounty hunter Fernando had told Zec and her about. What appeared to be concern for her brother was a disguised probe in his tracking of Maury McRae. Panic rose up in her and she regretted abandoning the scattergun. Relief flooded through her as a flock of frightened birds rose from the ground in the middle distance. Thankfully, that was a sign that told her Zec was returning home.

It was daylight when McRae awoke. The events of the night were a jumble in his mind that he strove to make sense of. Succeeding, at least in part, he recalled a young doctor increasing the pain he already felt by doing something to the wound in his side. As far as he had been able to ascertain, Max Nelson was the only other person in the room.

'It looked real bad when they brought him into the house, Doc. What's his chances?' Nelson had asked.

Unsure of either himself or his ability as a medical practitioner, the doctor had nervously turned his head to the rancher. 'He is in no danger whatsoever, Max. Though a previous wound has been opened, fortunately it has been expertly treated quite recently. I've tidied it up now, and he is a fine physical specimen. After two or three days rest he'll be fit for work again.'

'Thanks, Doc,' Max Nelson had said as he walked closer to the bed to stand looking down at McRae for some time before speaking. Then he said. 'I know that Reuben is responsible for this, McRae. But you can rely on me to deal with him. I'm not paying you to carry out personal vendettas on my ranch. Have you got that?'

Lacking the wherewithal to make a verbal reply, McRae signalled with his eyes. Seemingly satisfied, Nelson had walked away from the bed and out of the bedroom door. Now, as a Chinese woman entered the room carrying a tray of food for him, McRae was glad that he hadn't been in a fit condition to make Max Nelson any promises. It was his intention to settle his score with the hulking, brutal Reuben Nelson as scon as possible.

Pulling a chair up close to the bed, placing the tray on her lap, the Chinese servant gave him a friendly smile. Then she became serious as she carefully spoon-fed him with gruel that had an unpleasant taste.

'He appears to be a perfect gentleman, but I got the feeling that he's a *mal hombre*,' Zec Cordell remarked as Heather and he stood watching Durell ride away from their homestead.

'A very bad man, yes,' Heather agreed, shivering a little although it was already a warm day. 'He didn't give his name, but I'm sure he is the bounty hunter Fernando told us about.'

'That's for sure, Heather.'

The sun of a new day was now high in the sky, lessening

65

Heather's unease. She could handle the days fairly well, but dreaded the approach of twilight. Night made everything different. The darkness pours down, and the niggling little worries that sunlight holds off loom monstrous and misshapen. In daylight she had in one way been getting used to the threat presented by Max Nelson. But that wasn't the way she felt. Not the way she thought. Not down inside where it really counted. It was a kind of uneasy truce between herself and her worst fears.

'What do we do, warn Maury McRae?' she asked her brother as the departing Durell and his horse were made tiny by distance.

Shaking his head, Zec replied. 'No. We have enough to deal with protecting our home, and it's a real possibility that McRae is now a major part of what we're up against.'

Wanting to argue, Heather remained quiet. Nevertheless, she was convinced that Maury McRae would never do anything to harm them. So convinced that she wanted to protect him, she had to struggle to defeat the urge to plead with Zec to inform McRae of Durell's presence in the area.

Aware that would be a selfish thing to do, as her brother had enough worries to contend with, she decided to say no more on the subject. But McRae filled her thoughts as she returned to the chores she had abandoned when Durell had arrived.

Two days after treatment by the doctor, McRae was sitting on the edge of the bed eating a meal brought to him by the Chinese woman servant who had spoon-fed him soup up until then. Since feeling fitter, a question had been plaguing him. How do you tell a man that his son and stepson were stealing from him? That question troubled his conscience. In the short time he had been at the *Two Circles* he had not developed the slightest liking for Max Nelson, but he was on the rancher's payroll. That made loyalty to Nelson obligatory.

There were other considerations that prevented him from solving the problem. Though he owed a duty to Nelson, Heather Cordell had saved his life. Before he could come to any firm decision, he needed to learn exactly what part, if any, Zec Cordell was playing in the rustling of *Two Circles* beef. Tomorrow morning he would be back in the saddle, and would head out to determine Cordell's involvement before deciding what action to take.

He was surprised when the door of the room opened. Juanita stood there, leaning with a shoulder against the doorjamb. It was the first time he had seen her since being brought to the ranch house. Max Nelson had visited him often, and during one visit had repeated that he would be punishing his son for the assault on McRae, who must not seek revenge personally.

'I see you are able to sit up and take nourishment,' she remarked in her mildly mocking way.

'I thought you'd forsaken me. I had expected to see you before this,' McRae complained.

'I am a married woman,' she reminded him in tongue-in-cheek style. 'My dear husband has just taken himself off to Etheridge, so I thought that I'd find out how you are.'

'I'll be back in the saddle tomorrow.'

'A quick recovery,' she acknowledged. 'I believe the doc said that is due to the wound Reuben opened up having been professionally tended to in the first place. I didn't need ten guesses to realize that it was Heather Cordell who was responsible, seeing as Doc Faylen is the only other medically capable person within a hundred-mile ride.'

Though she had attempted to sound casual, there was a ring of jealousy in her tone that perturbed McRae. The way things were shaping up at the *Two Circles* ranch were worrying enough without Max Nelson's wife adding more worries. He admitted. 'That's right. I had to pull in at the Cordell place on the way here. But—'

The sound of hoofbeats had him fall silent as Juanita hurried over to look out of the window, to announce. 'It's Sheriff Wood.'

'Don't let him know that I'm here,' McRae made what was a half plea.

She turned to him, her brow corrugated by a frown. 'The sheriff is a clever man, McRae. I'd guess that the reason he is here is because he *knows* that you are here.'

FIVE

Putting his empty plate to one side, McRae stood and waited and fretted. His gunbelt was on a small table beside the bed, but there could be no question of gunplay in the ranch house, particularly with Juanita present.

The door opened then and she re-entered the room. Behind her, framed in the doorway, was an expensively dressed man wearing a silver star in the left lapel of his dark grey jacket. McRae immediately classed him as what he termed 'good sheriff'. A rarity in his experience, he was looking at a man who would have been in a decent walk of life had he not been called from the shadows by a lawless West. Self-assured, he moved in the smooth, effortless way of a fighting man.

'Howdy,' he greeted McRae, extending his right hand.

Clasping the hand, McRae wryly remarked. 'This is the first time I've shaken hands with a sheriff.'

'Could well be the last time,' Wood remarked with an amused grin.

'Are you giving me a message, Sheriff?'

'Not at all. You've done no wrong in my territory, McRae. In my reckoning, there'll be blood spilled in this valley soon enough. There's no need for you and me to add to it.'

69

'Then why are you here, Sheriff?'

Wood paused thoughtfully. 'Frankly, I'm not certain about that myself. I guess I'm trying to prevent trouble or at least limit it. To explain what I mean would have me speaking out of turn in front of Mrs Nelson.'

'Go ahead, Sheriff Wood,' Juanita invited. 'Whatever is happening around here won't have me taking sides. Not even my husband's side.'

'Thank you, ma'am. I appreciate being able to speak freely.' The sheriff turned to McRae. 'I understand that Max Nelson has hired you to deal with the gang rustling his cattle. I welcome that. The rustling has to be stopped, and you will spare me having to send out deputies that I could usefully employ elsewhere. All that I ask, McRae, is that you keep an open mind about the whole thing.'

'I don't understand?'

Wood hesitated once again. Then he spoke slowly, carefully. 'As everything is in a state of flux it's real difficult to explain at this time. It seems to me there's something serious building up in this valley. If I'm right, then it will fall to me to protect other folk here by going against Max Nelson.'

'Other folk like Heather and Zec Cordell?' McRae queried.

'Yes,' the sheriff confirmed. 'And Ernie Roderick and his family, too, of course. I've checked on your past, McRae, and I recognize that though you have a disregard for the law, that does not make you a mindless killer.'

'I sure hope that you haven't got me wrong, Sheriff.'

'If that were possible, we wouldn't be talking friendly-like as we are right now. I never doubt my own judgement, McRae. If I did so in your case, then Heather, Heather Cordell that is, would put me right.'

Surprised by this, having heard from Max Nelson of Wood's interest in Heather, McRae looked swiftly at the sheriff, whose lean and handsome face was inscrutable. He found it odd that Wood didn't seem in the least fazed by Heather having a keen interest in another man. Then the truth of the situation hit McRae hard. The sheriff would not regard a wanted outlaw as a rival where the refined Heather Cordell was concerned. That was a dispiriting realization.

'What exactly are you asking of me, Sheriff?' Things were becoming more and more complicated for McRae.

'It's hard to say exactly,' Wood replied. 'I guess what I'm trying to say is that if Zec Cordell and Ernie Roderick are involved in the rustling, which I very much doubt, then Max Nelson won't wait for me to enforce the law, but will have you drive them out of the valley to leave it open for him to do a deal with the railroad company that wants to lay a line through here.'

'I had no notion about a railroad,' McRae said, knowing now that this was what Juanita Nelson had been warning him of.

'I guess that explains why I came here. If Nelson tries to force these people out of the valley, he'll find himself up against me, and he's no great shakes with a handgun.'

'So he'll have McRae do his fighting for him,' Juanita blurted out.

McRae was sure that anxiety had Juanita voice her opinion without intending to. He and the sheriff looked in her direction. Wood asked, 'Is there something you think you should say, ma'am?'

'I think that you have said it for me,' Juanita answered. Having committed herself, she continued, 'I would put it more plainly, and say that the two things, putting an end to the rustling and Max Nelson's plans for Cottonwood Valley, are one and the same.'

'Quite so,' the sheriff agreed.

When he weighed what Wood was saying against what Max Nelson had told him when he had arrived at the *Two Circles* it made sense to McRae. Even so, he had a verbal agreement with Max Nelson, and needed to be absolutely certain before breaking that.

'I understand what you are saying, Sheriff Wood, and appreciate you coming here to say it,' McRae expressed his thanks. 'But I will go along with Nelson like I said I would, until when and if I find out for myself that you are correct.'

Accepting this with a shrug, Wood picked up his Stetson, ready to leave. 'That's your prerogative, McRae, and I admire your sense of loyalty. I'd advise that you don't take too long. I have no wish to face you, but you won't find me back away from a shootout between us if it comes to that.'

'You don't have to tell me that, Sheriff.'

Walking to the door, Wood turned to say. 'I forgot to say that Durell is in Gray's Flat. I wouldn't want to be facing you and have Durell shoot you in the back.'

'That wouldn't be Durell's way of doing things, Sheriff.'

'You're right. He'll make his showdown with you into some kind of circus, with the largest audience he can find. If he takes one step outside the law, I'll deal with him before he can get to you, McRae.'

'Durell's a dangerous man,' McRae warned. 'I don't want you to fight my fights for me, Sheriff Wood.'

'You have never needed anyone to do for you, Maury,' Wood said, using McRae's first name. 'Mrs Nelson says that she won't be taking sides whatever happens. That choice is not open to you, and neither is it your style. So make sure you join the right side.'

'Which is?'

'That's a question you won't need to ask when the time comes,' Wood predicted as he put on his Stetson and left the room.

Standing on the veranda of the *Double U* ranch house, a strengthening wind dishevelling his iron-grey hair, Ernie Roderick put an arm round his daughter's shoulders as he spoke. 'I'll be right proud to have you as a son-in-law, Zechariah, but this here ain't the right time. Let this thing with Max Nelson die down, then Elsa and me will welcome you into the family.'

'It's not going to die down, Ernie,' an unhappy Zec Cordell said. 'Any day now it's going to explode, and we'll be in the thick of it.'

'That's true, Dad,' Ellie Roderick, close to tears, gave her opinion.

'Then so be it, Ellie,' her father nodded gravely. 'If that's the way it's to be, then Zechariah will have his work cut out taking care of Heather and their place, and me and the hands will be busy protecting your ma, you, and the *Double U*. When the dust has settled, then me and your ma will give you the kind of wedding you deserve.'

'But we've done nothing, it's Max Nelson who's in the wrong, Pa,' Ellie protested. 'So let Sheriff Wood take care of this silly dispute.'

'The sheriff is just one man, Ellie, and Max Nelson's got his son Reuben, that Mexican fellow Sanchez, and more'n thirty riders on his payroll, and there's talk now that he's got himself a hired gun. We've got only Zec, Pete Goodson, and four other hands.'

'From what I hear, not one of us would stand a chance against McRae, Nelson's hired gun,' Zec warned.

'That's what young Pete said,' Roderick agreed. 'He saw this McRae *hombre* use his gun in town.'

'So what do we do?' Ellie asked sorrowfully. 'Move out of the valley before any of you get gunned down?'

'No,' Zec said fervently. 'We stay here and make a stand.'

Ellie shook her head. 'I won't let Zec go up against Nelson's hired gun, and I know that Heather won't, either.'

'I will if I have to,' Zec said firmly.

'We don't know what will happen until the time comes, if it does come,' a philosophical Roderick pointed out. 'Things have a way of happening different to what you expect.'

'Whatever way it happens, it's going to be a real bad time, Ernie,' Zec forecast.

'Like I said, we can't deal with it until it occurs, so there's no point in scaring the women with talk like this,' Ernie Roderick said resolutely. 'Ma and Heather will have tea waiting for us, so let's get inside and eat.'

McRae had ridden out in the morning with a definite plan in mind. He intended to pick up the tracks of the rustled herd where he had first found them. From there he would backtrack to locate where they had begun. That way he should be able to find the gang of cattle thieves with the next stolen herd of beef. Hopefully, Zec Cordell would not be among them. On discovering when they would next be moving beef down the trail, he would follow them.

After riding for an hour, he reined up his pony at a spot where ridges, valleys, gullies, hills, knobs and draws were all laid out in a vast basin. He looked back and saw the flat spread out behind, silent, vast, deserted, slumbering in the swimming white sunlight. Moving on, he reached the crest of the last rise and saw, spreading before him, a level many miles wide, stretching away in three directions. It was a grass plateau, but the grass was dry and lifeless, rustling under his pony's hoofs. There was an absence of trees, save for a post oak thicket skirting the northern edge, and it was toward this that he urged his pony.

At the rim, the plateau dropped sheer, as though sliced with a knife. A short distance from the base lay a narrow strip of water that flowed slowly in its rocky bed, winding around the base of a small hill to disappear between the buttes farther down.

His gaze swept down into a section of flat near the river. A small herd of cows, all with calves, was grazing there. Two riders slowly circled them to hold them in a tight group. Another cowpuncher was on foot, tending a fire beside which lay branding irons. Though he was exposed, McRae knew that the thicket behind made him close to invisible.

It was a puzzling scene that didn't have the trappings of a branding outfit. There was no wagon present. McRae reasoned that maybe it was off beyond a long range of flat hills that stretched for several miles. Yet that made no sense. Getting down from his pony, he walked the final few feet to the very edge of the plateau, dropping to his hands and knees to crawl the last few feet. As he got settled and looked down, one of the cowboys stretched up in his saddle to swing a rope. McRae saw the noose fall accurately over the head of a cow the man had selected. Pivoting his pony to drag the cow over on to its side, the man dismounted, ran swiftly to the fallen cow, and deftly wrapped a short rope around its hind legs.

The cow was hog-tied, the usual practice to prevent a cow from struggling during branding. It seemed that this was about to happen. Smoke from the fire curled lazily upward as the man there turned some branding irons. But the scene was all wrong for McRae. No ranch had cows running the range unbranded, especially when the cow has got a calf. Leaving the fire, the cowpuncher rushed toward the fallen cow. Reaching the side of the animal, the cowboy bent over it to press the red-hot irons against the bottoms of its hoofs. A thin wreath of smoke rose as the cow struggled frantically.

Now the scene took on meaning in McRae's mind. The trio of cowboys were stealing the calves, and burning the cows hoofs so that they couldn't follow when they ran the calves off. There was real good money in unbranded calves.

The second mounted cowboy was already twirling his rope over his head to lasso the next victim. There was something unusual about the man, and it took McRae only a short while to realize what it was. Instead of the customary wide-brimmed Stetson, the cowboy wore a bowler hat. The sight of it clicked a memory into McRae's head. When he first arrived at the *Two Circles* ranch, one of the hands riding in off the range had been a middle-aged, round-faced man, wearing a bowler hat. That was Dean Razzo, Sanchez's right-hand man.

The rustlers stealing Max Nelson's cattle were definitely his own employees. It seemed like both Fernando Wood and Juanita were mistaken about the rancher. McRae tried to recognize something about the other two men, but the distance was too great. Satisfied that they wouldn't be moving until the next day, he decided to move back a few miles along the trail the rustlers would take, and bed down for the night.

He intended to rise at first light and be at a high vantage point to view that area where the tracks had previously shown him one rider had gone off at a tangent towards the Cordell homestead. If Zec was to join the three men with the stolen calves somewhere along the way, then he was sure to make the detour home again. Once he had information of that kind, then he would know what he must do.

It was a sumptuous meal, a veritable feast made all the more enjoyable for Max Nelson by the knowledge that the three railroad executives sharing the table with him were paying for it. Yet his nerves were a little on edge. A deal had more or less been struck, but had yet to be sealed with his signature and that of Calumet McClurg, the railroad's head man.

Though having agreed a figure that was most favourable to Nelson, McClurg still had some reservations about the agreement. Silas Rayburn, the railroad's undersized, shifty-eyed lawyer, had caused the present stalemate by whispering these misgivings quietly into McClurg's ear. Eating noisily while Nelson exchanged meaningless pleasantries with a circling Miguel Morales, the hotel proprietor, McClurg was ready for further discussion when Morales moved away. Nelson hoped that this would be merely a matter of a few final details to be easily dispensed with.

McClurg thrust his bull neck toward Nelson. A heavy roll of fat swelled over his collar, and tiny red capillaries patterned his beefy face as he spoke forcefully. 'We have laid thousands of miles of track across America, Mr

Nelson, without so much as meeting even a lone dissenter, encountering any confrontations, nor hearing a single angry word. I don't doubt your word for a moment, but we need to be sure of the legal status of the other landowners in Cottonwood Valley. I understand that they number two, a small rancher and a homesteader?'

Harridan, the third member of the railroad team, nodded sagely and repeatedly in support of his colleague's prudent questioning. Rayburn, the lawyer, gave Nelson a sly, this-finicky-bickering-has-nothing to-do-with-me, smile. Nelson wasn't fazed by the fact that he was patently negotiating with a deceitful trio of men. In fact, he welcomed their trickiness. He found it easy to do business with people such as these. It was honest folk that he was unable to understand.

'That is true, Mr McClurg,' Nelson admitted. 'But this need not concern you in any way. The rancher and the homesteader have been rustling my stock for some considerable time. Evidence has been gathered that proves this beyond doubt, and the sheriff is ready to make his move. My compensation for loss of cattle will far exceed the value of the *Double U* ranch and the homestead combined. The legalities will be completed immediately now that the sheriff is in a position to make arrests, and is keen to do so. That may well be taking place as we speak.'

'I see,' McClurg said dubiously, bending sideways to take some papers from a case. Leafing through the papers on the table, he gave a gut-rumbling belch before saying, 'This is Sheriff Fernando Wood to whom you are referring, who I am given to understand is both a highly efficient and upright law officer?'

Cursing silently, an annoyed Nelson thought: this son of a bitch has checked out all the angles. That made it likely that the discrepancies in his scheme might well become apparent. The aloof, self-assured Fernando Wood had never concealed his dislike of him, which had Nelson doubt that the sheriff would take action against the Cordells and the Rodericks in any circumstances. He needed to do some quick thinking, to muddy the waters of negotiation with yet more prevarication. But McClurg and his two associates had been lying to him ever since he'd met them, so it came easy to give McClurg worthless reassurance. 'That's right. Fernando, who I'm proud to say is a close friend of mine, very close in fact, is the best.'

'If you don't mind, as it is' – McClurg took a gold watch from his pocket and consulted it studiously – 'only four o'clock, I would like us to go and speak with Sheriff Wood before completion. You understand that, with shareholders' money involved, we have to dot all the "I's" and cross all the "T's".'

'That is understandable, of course,' Nelson agreed, before employing his natural abilities as an accomplished actor. Then he gave a frustrated groan and banged the table with his clenched fist. 'Damn it. I forgot. Fernando has a large territory to cover, and he won't be back here in Etheridge for at least three days.'

Instantly suspicious, McClurg considered this for a long moment, then expressed his worry. 'There is nothing personal in this, Mr Nelson, no reflection of your character whatsoever. You are a truthful, straightforward, straight-talking gentleman with whom we have enjoyed doing business. But it is obvious that the final removal of these rustlers from the valley is out of your hands. There are situations that at times divert or deter even the most dedicated and courageous lawman. What if for some reason, the sheriff is unable to see his way clear to carry out his duties, and these two men retain their properties in the valley? We will have signed away a huge amount of other peoples' money, only to come to a halt.'

'I am absolutely confident that won't happen,' Nelson responded.

It was vital that this objection be dealt with swiftly. Sheriff Wood's three-day absence was Nelson's invention. For all he knew, Wood might be sitting in his office at that very moment. He was, however, certain that the railroad trio had believed what he had told them, and would not wish to remain in town for a further three days until the sheriff returned. The reluctance to commit was still very evident on the faces of the three men sat around the table with him.

'Rest assured, gentlemen,' Nelson advised them in a confident voice, 'that once our signatures are added to the agreement, you have nothing to fear. Should your fears prove to be well founded, which I swear to you they will not be, then it is I who stands to lose everything that I own. Every last cent. We will be entering into a legally binding contract. By signing the document I will be promising you the rights to every last inch of Cottonwood Valley. If Cordell and Roderick were to stay put, something that will not happen, then I will have reneged on the contract we are making. The law will give you full support when you invoke your right to sue me.'

McClurg looked to Silas Rayburn for a legal opinion, Rayburn exchanged glances with Harridan, and then all three stared fixedly at Nelson. Time slowed agonisingly for Nelson, who could see Miguel Morales seemingly heading back in their direction. Thankfully, a diner beckoned to the hotel proprietor. With that worry over, Nelson's biggest fear welled up inside of him. His dread was that

Sheriff Wood might come strolling into the restaurant at any moment.

McClurg turned his large head slowly to glance at Rayburn. The lawyer gave a barely perceptible nod. This was a signal that had the railroad boss extend a chubby hand to Nelson, and declare, 'We are satisfied, Mr Nelson. Let's drink to a mutually rewarding end to our negotiations, and then we will go to my room and sign the agreement.'

Shaking the proffered hand, Nelson offered up a silent prayer to a god he didn't believe in. Immensely relieved to have reached agreement, he now found himself fretting over the possibility of manipulating McRae in order to have the outlaw not only to drive the Cordells and the Rodericks from the valley, but also to rid the territory of the obstacle that was Sheriff Fernando Wood. The only difficulty in his scheme was that McRae was a sensitive, thinking man, not the cold-blooded brute one would expect someone living his kind of life to be.

It had become a regular daily event for Durell to take tea with Martha Tinkler. She was disposed to the company of a gentleman who could tell enthralling tales of the doings of high society back East. She would sit agog across the table from him as he related the discussions he'd had with President Rutherford B. Hayes. Each incident he related had her ask a succession of questions, many of which forced him to conjure up answers in his imagination. Durell skilfully hid the fact that he was bored beyond belief by the elderly woman, for she was a mine of information.

'I met Miss Cordell a day or two ago,' he said, smiling with pretend delight as he took one of the fresh-baked cakes she proffered. 'You say that she is a doctor?'

Topping up his cup, she waited until placing the teapot back on the table before replying. 'I don't believe that she sat her exams, having decided to come out here to help her brother. Nevertheless, she is obviously highly skilled. Several women in and around Gray's Flat have good reason to be grateful for her abilities as a midwife.'

'She did strike me as a remarkable lady. Quite capable of treating this injured drifter you told me about, Miss Tinkler.'

'Oh yes, indeed,' her eyes went distant as she imagined the situation they were discussing. 'I believe that he was badly hurt, but Heather tended his wound with most impressive expertise.'

'He was a fortunate young man,' Durell commented. 'I don't think that he was still there when I called at the Cordell homestead on one of my little tours of the area.'

'Oh no, he wouldn't have been. They say that he was fit to ride away within days, Mr Durell.'

'Never to be seen again,' Durell surmised poetically and purposefully.

Amused by his reference to the transitory nature of the West's population, she politely corrected him. 'That isn't the case, Mr Durell. I'm given to understand that the young man in question went only as far as the *Two Circles* ranch, where he now works for Mr Nelson.'

To cover his excitement at having gained this information, Durell curried favour by asking a question that had a built-in compliment. 'I wonder if I may be greedy and have one more of those delightful cakes of yours, Miss Tinkler?'

Pleased by this, the spinster held out the plate for him just as the black woman she employed on a part-time basis came into the room.

'What is it, Bella?' Martha Tinkler enquired.

'I am sorry to trouble you, Miss Tinkler, but there is a gentleman here who wants to see Mr Durell.'

Instantly alert, Durell regretted having left his gun in his room. The benign atmosphere of a hotel of modest size had seduced him into neglecting his always rigid regimen of self-protection. It had seemed silly to consider he might meet trouble in Miss Tinkler's house, but right then, being unaware of anyone who might have a non-threatening reason to call on him, he was convinced that he would.

'Do you know the gentleman's name, Bella?' Martha Tinkler asked, adding in a slightly annoyed tone, 'Mr Durell and I are having tea.'

'Yes, Miss Tinkler,' Bella stammered nervously. 'It is Mr Max Nelson.'

Turning to Durell, her eyes opened wide by surprise, Miss Tinkler gasped. 'Now isn't that a coincidence, Mr Durell. We were speaking of Mr Nelson just minutes since.'

Aware of the tension draining from him, Durell stood ready to meet the owner of the *Two Circles* ranch. As a man accustomed to having to make his own luck, it was a pleasant experience for him to have good fortune present itself unbidden.

SIX

'I must admit that your proposition interests me, Mr Nelson,' Durell said when Miss Tinkler had left the two of them alone in the dining room. 'Nevertheless, and I say this with the greatest respect, I am made suspicious by the fact that you are offering, on a day yet to be arranged, to produce Maury McRae for me here in Gray's Flat. I ask myself why you should make such a proposal. Are you seeking a percentage of the reward on this outlaw?'

'Most definitely not.'

'There is no taste in nothing, Mr Nelson, so you must have a reason for approaching me,' a frowning Durell said. 'You will appreciate that someone in my profession is far from popular, and needs to be cautious at all times. Therefore, I need to know more before I will even consider your offer.'

Indecision made Nelson hesitate. He looked around the room as if taking an interest in the decor, while Durell became increasingly impatient. Sensing this, Nelson cleared his throat noisily before speaking.

'I am a man of importance in this territory, a man highly respected by both businessmen and ordinary citizens alike. As the proprietor of a large ranch I provide employment for a considerable number of people. I have a need to protect my good standing, and have to be extremely cautious in all my dealings. I have an impeccable reputation in this territory, Mr Durell. That is why I must not get closely involved in this matter.'

'Closely involved!' Dwell gave a snort of disgust. 'If I accept your proposition, it will be my finger that pulls the trigger, but you will be equally responsible for his death when McRae is lying in the dust of that street out there. I will do my utmost to protect your precious reputation, but though my profession is frowned upon in general, I am personally regarded as a man who has never taken unfair advantage of any criminal whom I have brought to justice. So I, too, must avoid anything that is likely to tarnish my reputation. So either you tell me what is in it for you, or walk out of that door and don't come back.'

'McRae is working for me right now,' Nelson reluctantly explained. 'I took him on—'

'As a hired gun,' Durell interrupted him.

'That is not so,' Nelson's denial was bolstered by a vigorous shaking of his head. 'My reason for hiring McRae is to have him deal with the people who are rustling my beef.'

Walking to the door of the room, Durell opened it to check that Miss Tinkler was not eavesdropping outside. Satisfied, he walked back. Raising a hand, palm forwards to prevent Nelson from speaking, Durell said, 'I have to be fair and stop you there to tell you what I have already figured out. Not so very long ago I was a politician, a congressman, so I am conversant with deviousness and corruption of every kind. Added to that, since residing in Gray's Flat I have carried out considerable research.'

'What are you trying to tell me?' Nelson asked nervously.

Durell replied heatedly, his voice harsh. 'I am not *trying* to tell you anything, Nelson. I am about to tell why you have come to me. You hired McRae to chase a small rancher and a homesteader out of Cottonwood Valley. You want the whole valley to yourself so as to do a lucrative deal with a railroad company. Since I've been on Maury McRae's trail he's been so involved with running that he has had no time for robbing. He needs money so bad that you assume he'll do exactly what you ask of him.

'Your problem is Sheriff Fernando Wood, who is likely not to give you his blessing unless your actions against this rancher and settler are legally watertight, something which they can never be. So you'll need to have McRae gun down the sheriff. Fernando Wood is fast, but McRae is even faster, and that is really saying something. With Sheriff Wood out of the way, you want to use me to protect your impeccable reputation by taking care of McRae for you. Isn't that the truth, Mr Nelson?'

'What you say is—' an ashen-faced Max Nelson stammered.

'Don't waste my time arguing,' Durell butted in. 'Listen to me. At some time in the near future, you will want McRae dead. I want McRae, and you are in a position to bring him into Gray's Flat on one pretext or another. I will agree to that, and do what I have to do, if I have your promise to deliver McRae to me.'

'You have my promise,' Nelson assented, and then tried to recover at least a modicum of self-respect. 'You will forgive me if I don't shake on the deal. I just cannot imagine myself shaking the hand of a bounty hunter.'

With a disarming smile, Durell responded. 'I thank the good Lord for that. There is no way I could bring myself to shake the hand of a coward.'

*

Shortly after daybreak, McRae stood gazing down, eyes shaded from the orange-red glare of the rising sun by the wide brim of his hat, at the desolate, silent world that swept away from the base of the hill on the crest of which he had spent the night. Turning his head in the direction of the sun of a new day, he could see for miles to the east. There was no movement, no sign of the rustlers heading his way, herding the stolen calves toward a destination he could only guess at.

With time to spare, he strolled leisurely from the edge of the hill to where his pony stood, rested and fit for what would probably be a long day's ride. Swinging up into the saddle, he allowed his pony to choose its own course down the slope through small, loose stones. He reined up on reaching level ground. Still in no hurry, he sat relaxed in the saddle, looking about him. He was about to urge his pony on again, when some impulse moved him to glance down at sandy earth through which yellow-flowered weeds thrust up, nodding to the slight breeze. Eyes blinking in surprise, he swore aloud as he read the signs that told him he had made a wrong assumption the previous day. The rustled calves had passed through here during the night, while he had slept high above the trail.

Dismounting, he did an intense study of the tracks. What he discovered perturbed him greatly. Though he had witnessed three men burning the hoofs of the cows the previous day, four riders had passed here during the night. McRae tried but failed to dismiss the probability that the fourth man could be Zec Cordell.

Urgently needing to catch up with the rustlers, he mounted up fast and spurred his horse. Even so, when nearing the curve in the trail where one rider had split off the last time he was there, he slowed his horse. Reluctant to learn whether he was right or wrong about Cordell's involvement in the theft of cattle, he forced himself to study the ground. It took only minutes for him to learn the worst.

One rustler had again ridden off alone in the direction of the Cordell homestead. Hoping to discover that he was mistaken, McRae moved a few yards along the single track. Double-checking, he had to accept that his first assessment of the situation had been correct. It had to be that Zec Cordell had once more temporarily left the gang to ride home and ensure that the sister he had left on her own was safe and well, a sister for whom McRae now felt massive sympathy. Heather could not know that her brother was involved in stealing cattle, for she would never allow it to happen.

Riding on, McRae found his reasoning confirmed when he reached a point along the rustlers' trail where a single-horse track came from the direction of the Cordell place to rejoin the three other riders. This made McRae decide to continue following the rustlers until, as it was logical to presuppose, they arrived at the *Double U*, the Roderick ranch.

An hour later he reached the entrance to a valley. Urging his pony on a little way, he pulled it to a halt on the flat, rock-strewn top of an isolated outgrowth of earth surrounded by a sea of sagebrush and dried bunch grass. It was a wide, yellowish-brown valley, luxuriant – a golden-brown sweep that nestled between some hills, peacefully alluring.

The scenery had a deep affect on McRae. Emotion threatened to overcome him as the serenity of the place relaxed his mind. Like a drowning man is said to experience a rapid replay of his life, so did McRae watch a series of images of his past march past in all its bleakness, its emptiness. Worried that this mental aberration may portend his imminent death, he forced himself out of the daydream that was becoming a nightmare, and rode on remembering that when delirious from a gunshot wound he had told Heather Cordell that he had reached the end of his last trail. Had that been an omen? That possibility bothered him greatly.

Later, though he had covered some distance and had left the valley behind, the weird mental happening was still troubling him. Five miles into the distance, at a point where the river curved sharply, rose the roofs of a few ranch buildings It had to be the *Double U* ranch owned by Ernie Roderick, Zec Cordell's friend, and most likely his partner in crime.

That was something that he would soon be able to prove or disprove, he thought as he rode on. His past, that a short while ago had abruptly and harrowingly done an explicit rerun through his head, was fading fast now. It was replaced by an angel-like vision of Heather, and tantalizing thoughts of what might have been. So engrossed was he in this pleasurable reverie, that he was within one and a one half miles of the Roderick ranch before noticing that he was no longer following the tracks of the rustlers and calves.

Reining his pony about, he had ridden only a few hundred yards before picking up the tracks where they had veered to the north. McRae halted, and sat loosely in the saddle as he considered this new and unexpected turn of events. On his reckoning, bogus evidence had been produced to show Cordell and Roderick were behind the rustling. A false trail had been laid to the Cordell homestead, and then it had been made to appear that the main trail led to the *Double U*, before it had turned away before reaching the ranch.

His first inclination was to continue following the rustlers, but he couldn't be sure that it was necessary. In a short space of time he had reached two contradictory conclusions. The trickery involved in laying a false trail to the *Double U* didn't necessarily mean that the single horse track to the Cordells' home and back to the main trail was also a ruse. But he accepted that was nothing other than wishful thinking. There was nothing else to prove now, and he had the beginning of a plan in mind. But could he turn back, making a return to the *Two Circles* without determining the rustlers' destination? Yet to do so would be self-defeating. He was telling himself this when his horse suddenly became restless, swinging its head and snorting.

The possibility of a threat to his survival immediately alerted McRae. Long experience from living in a dangerous world had his body slip smoothly and naturally into a prepared-for-action mode. Some two hundred yards distant, a rider sat motionless in the saddle, staring at him.

Wheeling his pony and facing the man, whose appearance was made blurry by the late-afternoon, varicoloured radiance coming from the far-distant mountains. McRae's first impression was a vague one, no more than a dark Stetson and a yellow bandanna. Then the rider took on a slightly familiar form. This puzzled McRae, as he knew very few people in the territory, and he could recognize nothing about the menacing horseman up ahead. Then a clue came to him, soon to be joined by more recall that brought back a memory. The rider had the looks of the man who had ridden into the Cordell homestead the evening that he and Zec had been sitting on the veranda. That was it! McRae dug his heels into his pony to send it at a chop trot closer to the other man.

Searching his mind for the rider's name, it came to McRae as he pulled his pony up and said by way of a neutral greeting. 'You're Pete Goodson.'

'What are you doing in these parts, McRae?' There was nothing impartial in the snarled response.

'I was just—' McRae began.

'You ain't welcome here,' Goodson said as he dismounted. Hands at his sides, his right hand hovering above his holstered gun.

'There's no call for this, *amigo*,' McRae said calmly and quietly.

'I'm not your friend, McRae.'

Mystified by the hostility, McRae guessed the young cowpoke thought he was there to make a move on the Rodericks. Yet Goodson didn't have the serene calm or the easy assurance, the unstudied nonchalance, that seemed to be the inherent birthright of the gunfighter, the kind of hard man McRae was accustomed to facing in a gunfight. Goodson was just a cowpuncher forcing himself to carry out a heroic act to protect his employer and friends. McRae admired his courage.

'Just don't make a move of any kind, Goodson,' McRae cautioned. 'I'm going to ride round you and be on my way.'

'Dismount, McRae, or I'll blast you out of the saddle.'

'Don't be foolish, kid.'

'I ain't a kid, McRae. Get down, or I'll do as I said.'

It was plain that Goodson was serious, and McRae climbed slowly down from his pony. He stood facing the straw boss, holding his hands high, away from his gun.

'What now, Goodson?' he asked.

'Slap leather whenever you're ready to.'

'I'm not going to draw on you, kid,' McRae said, now able to see a trace of nervousness in Goodson. But if that developed it would make the cowboy unstable. Added to the determination he was showing, that would make him increasingly dangerous.

'Then I'll do a count of three.'

'Don't make me kill you,' McRae pleaded, but it was as if Goodson hadn't heard him.

He started to count. 'One . . . two . . .'

'My name is Harridan.'

As the man beside him spoke, Sheriff Wood turned slowly from the bar in the Four Aces saloon. Having only arrived back in Etheridge ten minutes earlier, he was weary and needed nothing more than a quiet drink before retiring for a peaceful night's sleep. Consequently, he didn't welcome this approach by a stranger. He found himself facing a well-dressed, middle-aged man who was painfully thin. Apprehension giving him a false appearance of diffidence, his lean face creased into a smile in an attempt at easing the sheriff's obvious annoyance.

'Is your name supposed to mean something to me?' the sheriff asked pointedly but not impolitely.

'No, sir, I guess that isn't,' Harridan admitted, his smile becoming smaller and changing from sociability to embarrassment. 'I am with the railroad company. Three days ago, my associates and I reached a business agreement with Mr Max Nelson here in Etheridge. I agreed to remain behind pending your return to

Etheridge, Sheriff.'

'I am a lawman, not a businessman, Mr Harridan.'

'I am aware of that, of course, Sheriff,' said an uncomfortable Harridan. 'The thing is, the said agreement gives us the right to bring our line through Cottonwood Valley. However, there was a minor hitch, as it were, with regard to two other landowners in the valley, but Mr Nelson set our minds at rest on that by assuring us that you have, or will shortly, arrest the other two residents in the valley. I understand that they have been stealing Mr Nelson's livestock, and will have to surrender their land to him in compensation. Now, Sheriff Wood, permit me to purchase a drink for you.'

'When you hear what I have to say, Mr Harridan, you will have no wish to buy me a drink.'

These words from the sheriff had Harridan stop part way in the act of taking his wallet from his pocket. Freezing as if suddenly paralyzed, his face registering extreme shock, he gasped. 'I am afraid that I don't understand, Sheriff.'

'Oh, it's quite simple, Mr Harridan. I have no evidence that either Zec Cordell or Ernest Roderick, the only two landowners in Cottonwood Valley apart from Max Nelson, have stolen any cattle. In fact, knowing both men as hardworking, upstanding citizens, I would be stunned if either of them has ever stolen as much as a double eagle. I can only suggest that you and your associates cancel the agreement you have with Max Nelson.'

'It's too late for that,' Harridan, badly shaken, his lips quivering, said in a hoarse half-whisper. 'We have committed a huge sum of shareholders' money, Sheriff.'

'Then the solution is to go to law. We have a court here in Etheridge at which Judge Baldwin sits once every month. I have no reason to doubt what you say, so Max Nelson has shown a total disregard for the truth when entering into a contract with you. From what you tell me, your company has nothing to fear. I suggest that you return to your headquarters and start to prepare a case. The judge will be here in just under two weeks.'

'We can't delay the railroad for that long, Sheriff.'

'Then first file your case against Nelson, then find another route round Cottonwood Valley, and retrieve at your leisure the money paid to Max Nelson,' Wood suggested.

'If only it were that simple,' Harridan groaned.

Though feeling some sympathy, Wood was unable to keep a touch of cynicism from his voice when he said, 'You look unwell, Mr Harridan. Permit me to purchase a drink for you.'

But the railroad executive was already hurrying to the door of the saloon, and most likely hadn't heard the invitation.

'. . . three.'

Nervousness had Pete Goodson shout the final number, his face chalk white as his hand went down to his holstered gun. Remaining absolutely still, McRae waited for the cowboy to realize how hazardous was the situation. Personally, he had no worries. He knew that he could afford to delay until after Goodson's fingers had curled round the butt of his six-shooter, and still beat the youngster to the draw. The whole thing was so frighteningly easy that he was being forced to commit murder.

But the too bright blue eyes of the *Double U* straw boss showed that he knew that he had gone beyond the point of no return, and that knowledge was terrifying him. Even so, he had no intention of backing down. Regretting the necessity to do so, McRae went for his gun and fired before Goodson's .45 had cleared the holster. He had deliberately shot low, aiming for the young cowboy's right thigh.

Standing upright, face expressionless, eyes bulging, staring at McRae for a long moment, Goodson then fell over sideways as his right leg gave out on him.

Reaching behind his neck, inside of his shirt, McRae drew a knife from a sheath before hurrying to kneel beside the cowboy. Goodson was conscious, his face twisting in agony as the pain of the bullet wound kicked in. Slashing open the trouser leg, McRae looked at the blood-pumping wound. He gave a grunt of satisfaction as a bloody bullet fell out of the sliced-open trousers.

'It's OK, Goodson,' he assured the injured man. 'There's no serious damage. The bullet went through the flesh of your thigh, but you're bleeding real bad.'

'For a man who did that shooting in town,' Goodson, relieved that the danger was over and that, unexpectedly, he was still alive, exclaimed in a croaking, quavering voice, 'you're sure as hell one poor shot.'

'I told you that I didn't want to kill you,' McRae grinned as he reached up to untie the cowboy's yellow bandanna.

Wrapping the bandanna around Goodson's thigh above the bullet wound, he tied it tightly. Glancing around, he picked up a short branch that had snapped off a nearby tree. Breaking off the few twigs and leaves growing from it, he wiped the stick on his trousers before pushing it between the bandanna and the cowboy's leg, and twisting it to make a tourniquet.

'That will slow down the bleeding,' he told Goodson.

'But you urgently need medical help.'

'I'll never make it all the way into Gray's Flat,' the cowboy groaned.

'I know that. I'm going to help you on to your feet now, then get you up into the saddle. Along the way I'll have to release the tourniquet at intervals to allow the blood to circulate. If I don't, that leg won't ever be any use to you again.' It worried McRae that Goodson's face was now a peculiar kind of translucent white.

'You know a lot about these things,' Goodson commented, his voice growing weak.

'I've practised on myself a lot,' McRae said, and he wasn't joking.

'I have to admit that you were right, McRae; I was being foolish,' Goodson apologized, the effort to do so drastically draining his strength. 'I didn't have a chance against you. I guess I should thank you for sparing my life.'

'I won't have spared it if we don't get you to a doctor soon,' McRae said grimly.

'Where are you taking me?'

Reaching under the cowboy's arms, McRae pulled him to his feet before answering. 'To have Heather Cordell fix you up.'

Propped against a tree while McRae went to fetch his horse, Goodson was so feeble that he began to slide down. McRae caught him and, having to treat the wounded man roughly out of necessity, he put an arm over his shoulder and moved Goodson close to his horse and half pushed, half hoisted him up into the saddle.

'I'll take the reins, you just cling on to the pommel with both hands,' he instructed.

Groaning with pain, sweat dropping from his face, Goodson gasped. 'Did you say the Cordell's place?'

'I did,' McRae confirmed as he mounted his own pony.

'Zec . . . will . . . Zec will shoot . . . you before you get . . . within . . . within ten miles of his place,' Goodson managed to say, painfully.

'Then I guess you'll have to take care of me,' McRae advised drily, reaching for the reins of Goodson's horse and moving away.

'It ain't going to work.'

Reuben Nelson shouted angrily at his father, who had returned from Etheridge in a foul mood. Barely speaking to his wife, he had summoned his son. Now the tempers of both men had flared to a peak. Feeling nothing but contempt for both the father and the son, Juanita was just a disinterested spectator.

'We have to make it work, Reuben, and we will.'

'McRae has been here some time now,' Reuben complained, 'yet he still hasn't come up with any solid proof. It's all there, right before his eyes. I figure that he just don't want to see it.'

Knowing why this was so, that McRae would have no wish to cause Zec and Heather Cordell, especially Heather, trouble, Juanita remained silent.

Incensed by his son's attitude, Max Nelson spat out his words. 'You are one danged stubborn cuss, Reuben. McRae is out there right now, and I'll allow he'll be back soon. Then I'm sure he'll be able to tell us what we want to hear.'

'What if he don't?'

'Can't you ever look on the bright side, Reuben?' Max Nelson complained, secretly dreading that his son was right.

'All right, I'll look on the bright side. McRae will be

back, that's for sure.'

'That's better, son.'

'But what if he ain't got proof that Cordell and Roderick are stealing our beef?'

'Reuben, Reuben, what can I do with you?' a frustrated Nelson moaned. 'I have a back-up plan.'

'Foolproof?'

'Absolutely, son.'

'Then tell me.'

'McRae doesn't have a dime to his name, son, and he's got Durell on his trail,' Max Nelson began. 'Nobody can survive without money, chiefly a man being hunted down like a dog. I need to get Cordell and Roderick out of this valley fast, so I'll pay McRae whatever it takes.'

'Ain't you overlooking one important thing, Pa?'

'Fernando Wood,' Max Nelson said rather than questioned. 'I'd be right foolish to forget the sheriff, Reuben. I'm prepared to pay McRae enough to take care of him, too.'

Not wanting to hear anything further, Juanita got up from her chair and quietly left the room.

SEVEN

Concern for the wounded man had McRae halt on coming to a shelf-rock, beside which grew a twisted gnarl of scrub-oak brush. It was a place favoured by a sun that was now lingeringly and reluctantly withdrawing as the long shadows of twilight crept closer. Yet the romance and mystery of the place was lost on McRae, whose interest lay wholly in the soft sand as he dismounted and helped the now extremely weak Pete Goodson down from his horse.

'There's not far to go now,' he said consolingly to the groaning man as he laid him down on the sand. 'But I need to slacken this tourniquet for the last time, *amigo*.'

Doubting that Goodson could hear him, let alone reply, he eased the tension of the tight bandanna. It worried him greatly when no blood oozed slowly from the wound within the time he had expected it to. Then, taking him by surprise, it suddenly gushed out and continued spurting from the wound with alarming force. Concerned now by the amount of blood that Goodson was losing, which he could ill afford to lose, he did some quick thinking.

Untying his own bright-green bandanna, McRae pulled it swiftly off and folded into a pad, which he pressed hard against the wound. Sitting back on his heels, he kept the

99

pad against the wound. Relieved by the staunching of the flow of blood, he waited to allow time for the circulation to resume in the rest of the leg. Eventually satisfied, he knelt beside his patient, holding the pad in place with one knee while he retightened the tourniquet.

Getting the limp body of Goodson back up into the saddle was a struggle, but he managed it and was soon on his way. Made uncertain by the darkness in terrain that was strange to him, and fearing that he might not be in time to save Goodson's life, he breathed out a whistling sigh of relief as he caught sight of a corner of the Cordells' cabin. Moving slowly so as not to cause Goodson additional distress, he could see a section of the corral fence, and the entire small barn.

Opposite to the cabin was the great stretch of flat country that was rimmed on three sides by a fringe of low hills, hills that he remembered from the time when he had sat on the veranda with Heather. There was one particularly tall hill behind the crest of which the setting sun had gone down with a memorable shimmering of a saffron light in late evening. Strangely, this recall made McRae, a man who had never known a home, homesick.

Grateful for the growing darkness as he rode closer, McRae could see the glow of the oil light in a window of the cabin. Maybe Goodson had been foolhardy, but had been made so by the situation in the valley. He hadn't deserved to be shot, but had left McRae with no option. Originally glad that his bullet hadn't damaged the youngster's thighbone, that now seemed preferable to it having ripped open an obviously important blood vessel in the leg of the straw boss.

Reining up within thirty yards of the homestead, McRae dismounted. He paused in deliberation, wanting to take

Goodson in, to explain what had happened, to see Heather again. But he remembered Goodson's feebly voiced warning that Zec Cordell would gun him down on sight. The way things had shaped up, the homesteader would be right to do so. He had to protect his sister and his home.

Walking back to stand by Goodson's horse, he placed the reins in one of the semi-conscious man's hands. He advised. 'Just allow your pony to walk, Goodson. My guess is that it will keep going straight to the cabin, but I'll stay here long enough to be sure.'

Goodson mumbled an unintelligible reply as McRae slapped the pony's rump lightly to send it off at a walk. Then he withdrew into the deepest shadows to stand watching the pony, with its rider slumped sideways to the left in the saddle, approach the cabin. He held his breath on two occasions when the pony veered slightly first to the left and then to the right, before getting back on course. At one time the pony came to a halt. After long, harrowing moments for McRae, it then went on its way once more. He guessed that the pony had recommenced walking of its own volition, as its rider was in no fit state to urge it on.

More tense moments passed, then McRae saw a light that told him the door of the cabin had opened. Though it was only lamplight, there was sufficient illumination for him to distinguish Zec Cordell stand facing the approaching horseman with a rifle held at the ready.

Content that Zec Cordell would recognize his friend before firing the rifle, McRae went to his own pony, swung up into the saddle and rode off slowly so as not to create the sound of hoofbeats in the quiet of night.

'Who is it, Zec?' Heather called fearfully from the cabin doorway.

The silence that followed, made menacing by the night, frightened her. The steady pound of hoof beats had alerted Zec and her. Made apprehensive by the dangerous state of affairs in Cottonwood Valley, her brother had grabbed the rifle and immediately gone outside. She hadn't realized that she had stopped breathing until she heard Zec answering her.

'It's Pete, Pete Goodson,' her brother replied, placing his rifle against the cabin wall. 'He's been shot. I'll need you to help get him inside.'

With Heather at his side, Zec freed Goodson's left foot from the stirrup, then went round to the other side of the horse to prise the right foot free. A cry of alarm from his sister made Zec realize that by releasing Goodson's right foot he had caused the injured man to topple to the left. He ran rapidly round the pony to push Heather away before the falling man would crush her. He managed to get a hold on Goodson, but the momentum of the falling body overbalanced him, and he crashed to the ground with Goodson on top of him.

Heather rolled the wounded man off her brother, and pulled Zec up on to his feet. The effort left her exhausted and unable to help Zec, who put his hands under the wounded man and dragged him into the cabin and lay him on the floor.

'How bad is he?' Zec enquired as his sister dropped to her knees beside their friend.

'It's not good. He's lost an awful lot of blood,' she reported, as she opened the long slit in the trouser leg. Her brow corrugated in puzzlement. 'This is odd, Zec. Someone has applied a tourniquet.'

'Probably saved his life.'

'Made an admirable attempt at doing so,' she partly agreed.

Shocked, Zec asked. 'You mean—'

'It will be a miracle if he survives, Zec.'

Dawn was breaking when McRae got back to the *Two Circles* ranch. Riding in, he passed a few of the hands carrying out mundane chores. Totally disinterested in him, they didn't even glance up as he went by. The place seemed deserted otherwise. A practically empty corral told him that most of the cowpunchers were out on the range. That was disappointing. He had a score to settle with Reuben Nelson, and was in a hurry to give vent to his frustrations on the powerfully built son of a rancher. As he drew closer, the ranch house door opened and Max Nelson stepped out as if he had been forewarned of his imminent return. The rancher stood waiting for him to return, his stance belligerent.

Still distressed by having been forced to shoot Pete Goodson, the sight of the avaricious, power-crazy rancher increased McRae's bad humour as he rode up to him.

'Well?'

That curt question was Nelson's only greeting. Keeping the rancher waiting, McRae wheeled his pony slowly in an arc, dismounted in a leisurely manner, and took his time in tethering the pony to the hitching rail outside the house.

Losing his patience, an angry Nelson strode up to him, to repeat his one-word question. 'Well?'

'Well what?' McRae drawled, taking the makings from his shirt pocket.

'I won't stand for insolence from those on my payroll, McRae.'

'I'm not being insolent,' McRae responded, a moving curtain catching his attention. Juanita was looking out at

103

them. Her gaze was unwavering as her eyes met his in a sharp, brief struggle. A struggle cut short by him looking away. Feeling the dominant personality of the woman, he needed to escape the effect it had on him. Concentrating on rolling a cigarette for a time, he then continued. 'I was just trying to discover what you are asking me.'

'I want to know if you have found out who is rustling my stock.'

Needing a few moments to think, to finalize his plan, McRae struck a match on the rail and gave a brief nod as he lit his cigarette.

'Is that yes?' Nelson asked tetchily.

'It is.'

'I was right, wasn't I, McRae?'

Deliberately delaying his reply, McRae said, 'I guess so. All the signs point to the Cordell homestead and the *Double U* ranch.'

'I knew it!' Nelson crowed in satisfaction. 'You can prove this, McRae?'

'I tracked two stolen herds, and the same evidence showed up both times. I'll be willing to testify to that.'

'Great stuff.' Nelson slapped his thigh noisily. 'Now I can make my move, McRae.'

'When?' McRae asked casually.

'Two . . . no, three days. Most of the boys are up on the top range and won't be back until Friday. I want Reuben, Sanchez, and Dean Razzo with us.'

'I won't need help from them or anyone else to do the job you're paying me to do,' McRae objected.

'Maybe not, McRae. But like you say, I'm paying you. That makes me the boss. I'll do things the way I want to do them.'

'Fair enough,' McRae shrugged. Needing to know

more, he asked what he knew Nelson would regard to be a harmless question. 'What do you think we might come up against when we reach the *Double U?*'

Wearing a smug smile, Nelson shook his head. 'You have it wrong, McRae. We hit Zec Cordell first, and we'll hit him hard, real hard.'

This was what McRae had dreaded hearing, but needed to know. Flicking the butt of his cigarette through the air, he turned away from Nelson. He learned from a quick glance at the window that Juanita was no longer watching. As he was untying his horse, Nelson called to him.

'Don't stray far from the ranch over the next few days, McRae. It may have to be at short notice, and I want you here when I need you.'

'Don't fret yourself about that, Mr Nelson,' McRae replied, almost obsequiously. 'I'll be there.'

Having made a wrong prognosis, a shameful mistake for a medical person, delighted Heather in Pete Goodson's case. Incredibly, in her learned opinion, he had begun a slow recovery from the moment she had treated the bullet wound in his thigh. Throughout the twenty-four hours he had been at the cabin, he drifted in and out of conscious, never gaining complete awareness.

Watched by her fretful brother, Heather was checking on the bullet wound, wondering whether she should tell Zec of the discovery she had made. Its portent was so serious that she knew that she must share the knowledge. It would give Zec additional worry, but to leave him ignorant would mean he would be unprepared for the imminent outbreak of violence.

'That bandanna that was used to stop the bleeding from Pete's leg,' she said, pointing to where the

105

improvised tourniquet had been discarded on the floor.

'What about it?'

'It's Maury McRae's.'

'Are you sure of that, Heather?'

'Positive. The colour is both striking and very unusual.'

'You think that it was McRae who shot Pete?'

'That occurred to me, but why would he take care of him afterwards?' a mystified Heather asked.

'Good God!' Zec suddenly exclaimed. 'Pete's eyelids moved just then, Heather. He's coming round. I'll ask him.'

'No,' Heather protested. 'You mustn't, Zec. He's very weak.'

Excited by seeing Goodson's eyes open, Zec was not listening to her. He asked. 'Do you feel up to answering a question for me, Pete?'

An almost imperceptible nod of the injured man's head was good enough for Zec, who followed up his first enquiry with. 'Who shot you?'

Brother and sister sat waiting, the latter agonizing over the state Goodson was in as he battled to find the strength to reply. His first attempts were no more than hoarse, coughing sounds, but then he managed to form what could have been words in an incoherent hissing whisper.

Ashamed at being caught up in her brother's curiosity, Heather bent over the injured man, her ear close to his mouth as she asked. 'Could you say that again, Pete?'

Hearing the whisper repeated but still unable to decipher it, Zec looked at his sister, raising both eyebrows in a silent question. But it was to no avail.

Ashen-faced, Heather stood up and fled to the kitchen. She was shaking uncontrollably when Zec joined her. Placing an arm round her shoulders, he asked gently,

'What did he say, Heather?'

'You won't believe it any more than I do, Zec.'

'How can I know that until you tell me what it was?'

Heather's lips moved tremulously, as she tried but failed to utter words. Then she blurted out, so loudly that it startled her brother, 'Maury McRae.'

'Good God!' Zec exclaimed.

'It can't be so.'

'I've never consider Pete to be a liar.'

'I know that he isn't, but he must be mistaken,' Heather unhappily agreed.

Frowning, Zec asked. 'The bullet that went through his leg was fired from a handgun, wasn't it, Heather?'

'Yes.'

'From what distance would you say it was fired?'

After a slight hesitation, Heather replied in a quiet voice. 'From reasonably close up.'

'So Pete would know who it was,' Zec told her gently. 'We have to face it. McRae is with Max Nelson now, and against us, Heather.'

'That's how it seems, I admit. But I just can't accept that he would do such a thing after what we did for him.'

'For our own sakes, Heather, we have to assume that he has. I've wanted to tell Ernie Roderick that Pete has been shot, but now he needs to know about this as well.'

'Then you must ride to the *Double U* right away, Zec,' Heather said resolutely. 'Tell him to send one of his men to Etheridge right away. We need to get Fernando here as soon as possible.'

'But I can't leave you here alone.'

'I have to care for Pete, and being alone doesn't worry me,' Heather assured her brother. 'What does frighten me is what is soon going to happen.'

Reaching for his coat, Zec concurred. 'You are right. I'll be as quick as I can, I promise.'

There was an expression of annoyance at being interrupted on Max Nelson's face as he looked up from the paperwork on his desk as his wife entered the room. 'What is it, Juanita?'

'There are two men here to see you. Real gentlemen by the look of them.'

'Did they give their names?'

'Yes, but I didn't quite catch them. I'm sorry,' Juanita apologized. 'But they did say something about a railroad.'

Jumping to his feet on hearing this, Nelson rushed roughly past his wife and dashed out of his study. Heading for the front door, the possibilities, all of them dire, of what this unexpected visit meant, ran chillingly and painfully through his mind. His nervousness increased a thousand-fold when he reached the open front door to find Calumet McClurg and Silas Rayburn, the railroad's lawyer, standing there.

'Good afternoon, Mr Nelson,' McClurg said amicably. 'Our Mr Harridan reports to us that there is a matter that we must discuss urgently.'

'I don't understand,' a genuinely baffled Max Nelson.

'May we come in?'

'Of course. Please forgive my lack of manners.'

Both of the railroad men flashed him an artificial smile, then followed him into his study. Gesturing towards two chairs, Nelson said. 'Please, gentlemen, be seated. What can I get you to drink?'

When they were seated, it was Rayburn who responded. The lawyer was no longer genial, the almost buffoon-like character he had appeared to be in the meeting at

Etheridge. He spoke forcefully. 'This is not a social call. We are here to demand an explanation. When we exchanged contracts you assured us that there was no impediment to you becoming the owner of all of Cottonwood Valley.'

'Our Mr Harridan has learned from Sheriff Wood that that isn't so,' McClurg interjected. Pointing an accusing finger at Nelson, Rayburn continued his verbal assault. 'The truth is that there is not the slightest possibility of you gaining full ownership.'

'Which means you are in breach of contract,' McClurg, his heavy-jowled face red with anger, thundered.

'I have prepared a writ ready for filing,' Rayburn said, holding up a slim leather case he had placed against his leg when sitting down.

'Yet we are reasonable men,' McClurg, who had rapidly mellowed, said in soft tones. 'All three of us here in this room are men of commerce, but, most importantly, we are gentlemen, men of honour. That is why we are here, to settle this in a mutually satisfactory manner. I am sure that we do not have to resort to the courts.'

Nelson was bewildered by the railroad men's double act. Words coming at him fast from two different directions stretched his nerves to breaking point. The intimidating attitude the pair had adopted on entering the house told him that they weren't here to renegotiate the Cottonwood Valley contract. They were about to deliver an ultimatum. Whatever it was that they wanted, he was in no position to give it to them. For the first time in his life he found himself in a situation in which he did not have complete control. He cursed McRae's delay in finding the evidence. Had he done so just a few days earlier, this problem wouldn't have arisen. His only chance was to bluster his way through the next hour, or however long it took to get these two bullies off his land.

'There will be no need to go to court,' Nelson said, wishing that he sounded more confident. 'Fernando Wood has a whole lot of territory to cover, much of it lawless. That is why I long ago put a contingency plan in action. Fearing that the sheriff would not be able to spare sufficient time to bring the valley's rustling problem to a conclusion, I hired an investigator of my own. I now have the necessary evidence.'

He did a surreptitious study of his visitors, and was daunted by the realization that they were not convinced. What would their reaction be, he wondered, should they discover that his 'investigator' was a wanted outlaw with a high price on his head.

'You say that you have the evidence, but you haven't explained how you will use it,' McClurg said dubiously.

Rayburn followed up quickly with, 'Should your evidence be sound, it would take time, time that we just don't have, for you to place it before Sheriff Wood and have him take action on it.'

'My contingency plan goes beyond collecting evidence, gentleman, and it will be completed this coming weekend, in a manner that you will find wholly satisfactory,' Nelson promised.

'Might we be so bold as to ask for details?' Rayburn sarcastically enquired.

'A comprehensive answer to Mr Rayburn's question would be appreciated, Mr Nelson,' McClurg added.

'You will have the answer, the go-ahead for your Cottonwood Valley project, on Monday, gentlemen.'

As if through some mental communication, both McClurg and Rayburn stood up, turned to look briefly at each other, then stared silently at Nelson. The long silence and the extended stare disturbed Nelson more than any of the preceding conversation had. Wanting to say something to break the silence, he could only endure the discomfort of it because there was nothing to say. It was Rayburn who spoke first.

'We will return on Monday, Mr Nelson,' he said amicably, but then added a threat. 'If you are unable to give our line a clear run through the valley then, it will make things very difficult for us. But I promise you, that if that should happen, we will make things far more difficult for you.'

They turned together with military precision, and left the room. Nelson followed them along the corridor, but they went out of the front door without speaking a word. Closing the door, he turned to find his wife standing a few feet away, an anxious expression on her face.

'Has something gone wrong, Max?' she enquired.

Not replying, he pushed past her to go into his study and slam the door shut behind him.

Suffering a relapse immediately after managing to speak McRae's name, Pete Goodson hovered between life and death. Spending an evening nursing him, Heather was exhausted when her brother returned at midnight.

'How is he?' Zec asked, looking worriedly down at the injured man's pallid face.

'Not good, Zec. His only hope is if his body can soon enough replace the blood he has lost.'

'And if it is unable to?'

With a tired shrug, Heather replied. 'Then he will die before morning.'

'Ernie has sent young Joe Fielding off to Etheridge,'

Zec said, changing the subject to ease the morbid thoughts they were sharing.

'How long do you think we will have to wait?'

'Not long, if Fernando is in Etheridge.'

'I pray that he is,' Heather said, then contradictorily hoped that her prayer would not be answered.

If, as was most likely, Pete Goodson died, Fernando Wood's first task would be to arrest McRae for his murder. Though starkly aware that McRae was a fugitive from the law, the sheriff had up to now declared no interest in him. Noticing Zec watching her, she felt her face burning. As brother and sister they were very close, and she was sure that he knew what she was thinking.

'McRae shot Pete, Heather,' he reminded her, proving her right.

'I know, but—'

'There can be no buts, Heather. Pete is a straw boss, no more no less, while McRae is a notorious fast gun. So it wasn't a shootout between equals. It was murder.'

Zec was right. There could be no argument. That fact upset her, made her very sad. She said listlessly, 'Go to bed, Zec. Get some sleep. You'll need it when all hell breaks loose in the valley.'

'No. You look real tuckered out, Heather. You go to bed. I'll sit with Pete. I'll call you if you're needed.'

'Thank you, but I can't do that. Fretting about him would prevent me from sleeping. I would never be able to forgive myself if something happened when I wasn't there.'

Understanding that it was pointless to argue, Zec made his way to his bed. As he went he turned his head to speak over his shoulder. 'Wake me if you need me, Heather.'

'I will. I promise.'

EIGHT

Climbing to the summit of a small hill, McRae tied his pony to a slender fir-balsam. Sitting on the trunk of a fallen tree, his gaze roved over the sweep of valley, dull and cheerless in the early dawn, with a mist rising out of it to meet and mingle and evaporate in the widespread colours of the slowly ascending sun. With the immediate future on his mind, he had ridden away from the ranch in search of solitude. He saw the world through the introspective eye of experience, recognizing that the original task of tracking down and dealing with a gang of rustlers had evolved into a bizarre situation. His high hopes of being paid by Nelson for simple work without involvement had been dashed. Now he knew that he could not leave Cottonwood Valley without a confrontation that would not only test his principles and his loyalty, but would leave him exposed to the bounty hunter who had tracked him relentlessly for so long.

For the past ten minutes he'd had a feeling that he was being observed, and he tensed, ready for action when a distant and sudden movement interrupted his thinking. Unable to be certain that he seen anything, he watched, motionless. Then he was positive. About half a mile away was a low hill topped with yucca, sagebrush, and octilla. He saw these desert weeds move as if ruffled by a breeze. But the air was still, and he saw something dark grey slink out from the weeds to show up clearly on the skyline. It was either a coyote or a wolf, and distance made it impossible for him to be sure which. But it was of no consequence. It was nothing for him to be concerned about.

Leaving the wild creature to follow its pursuits, his mind was once again busy with both memories and the ominous probabilities his tomorrows held. How much time passed by could only be estimated by the fact that he had rolled and smoked two cigarettes. Feeling secure in this lonely spot since discovering that it had only been a wild animal observing him, he permitted his self-preservation instinct to relax, which enabled him to think deeply.

So rapt was he in his thoughts that he had not noticed that the slinking creature he had seen creeping through weeds on the distant hill, had approached. It was no more than fifteen yards from him, crouching in the sagebrush and clumps of mesquite watching him with blazing, bloodshot eyes. Its dull grey hair, dank from morning dew, its yellow fangs bared in a silent snarl, the animal drooled from the exertion of stalking McRae for so long. Panting hard, it waited to pick the most favourable moment to attack.

All unaware, McRae was drawing on his third cigarette when the animal made its swift and soundless attack. By the time McRae felt the disturbance of air that was filled with the foul reek of the slavering beast as it sprang up from the ground, it was too late for any proper defence. Yet his reflexes worked superbly as always, and he swayed to the left. It was a good move, the best possible in the circumstances. But it was not wholly effective.

Aiming for the throat, the beast was thrown off target by McRae's defensive tactic. Nevertheless, he felt a single fang tear the side of his neck open as the drooling animal slammed into his shoulder as it flew past him. Though there was no pain, McRae could feel blood leaking from the gash in his neck.

On his feet now, he spun quickly to see the beast hit the ground behind him with a thud, its legs spread awkwardly and painfully apart. Recovering quickly, it whirled and with a snarl of rage leapt flying through the air in a second attack.

Prepared now, calm and cool, McRae went for his gun with the speed that had gained him fame far and wide. As if sensing danger, the animal twisted its body in mid air. But it gained nothing other than a modest veer to its right as McRae's six-shooter exploded with a terrific sound that reverberated in the morning air. Body creasing double as its leap was arrested, the beast then did a belly flop, landing heavily in front of McRae.

Though lying awkwardly, the animal, to McRae's annoyance, twisted its head, mouth open and slobbering blood flecked foam as it tried to sink its fangs in his leg. Taking a small step back, he kicked out hard with his right foot. His boot caught the animal under its jaw, breaking bones, snapping it shut, the force of the kick flipping it over on to its back. He could see a dark patch of blood on the chest of the beast close to its right foreleg. His shot had been slightly off target due to the animal's attempt to change course when in mid leap. But McRae made no mistake now. Still holding his gun, he looked into the maddened stare of its horrible eyes as he fired just once.

The bullet thudded into the skull of the beast between eyes that still glared at him. Some after-death reflex had it try to stand up. Making it only half way to being on all fours, it dropped to the ground, released a deep, body shuddering sigh, and lay still.

Holstering his Colt .45, McRae raised a hand tentatively to his neck. It came away with only a small amount of blood staining his fingers. The wound was far less serious than he had feared. Relieved, he was wiping the small amount of blood away with a handkerchief, when his ears caught the sound of hoofbeats. Alert once more, he saw three horsemen riding abreast, coming up the hill toward him.

When the trio topped the crest, McRae recognized Reuben Nelson, Sanchez, and Dean Razzo, complete with his distinctive bowler hat. Reining up no more than four yards away from McRae, all three dismounted. Nelson and Razzo remained stationary beside their horses, while Sanchez strolled up to McRae to stood looking down at the dead animal.

'It's Ike,' Sanchez said quietly, then turned his head towards his companions and raised his voice. 'It's Ike. He's shot your dog, Reuben.'

The big man strode angrily and accusingly up to McRae. He glanced sadly at the shot dog, then glared at McRae 'What in tarnation made you do such a cruel thing, McRae?'

When meeting a man for the first time, looking at him, meeting his eye, McRae always instantly knew whether he had won a friend or gained an enemy. Reuben Nelson had been his enemy since the can-shooting contest in Gray's Flat. Being close to Nelson now had all the hate he had ever felt for anyone in his life balloon up in him. It was so

116

powerful in its demand for violence, its pressure for him to attack the arrogant, detestable Reuben Nelson, so powerful that he was unable to speak.

'The critter attacked me,' he at last managed to say, not as an excuse but as a matter of fact.

'Ike hunted down wolves, coyotes and the like, not people,' Nelson said in disbelief, giving McRae a sickly, humourless smile.

McRae wasn't in the mood for a discussion with a man he deeply detested. He said challengingly. 'I'm not prepared to argue, Nelson. I guess it's right that we settle this and what has gone before between us, here and now.'

'I'm not toting a gun,' Nelson responded, spreading both arms wide to prove his point.

Carefully reaching to undo the buckle of his gunbelt with his left hand, McRae took the belt off and draped it over a low branch of a nearby tree. Then he told Nelson. 'Neither am I.'

'What's the matter with this hombre?' Nelson turned to Sanchez to ask.

But this was a trick. As he uttered the final word of his question, the big man swung back to aim a vicious kick at McRae's groin. However, not having anticipated that Nelson would fight fair, McRae was prepared. Grasping the booted foot with both hands before it could touch him, he twisted the foot and leg hard. Rewarded by a groan of pain from Nelson, McRae then pulled on the leg to unbalance his adversary. Then he held the sole of the foot against his stomach and rushed forwards. Pushed backwards, Nelson fell, landing flat on his back while McRae still held on to the leg, twisting it once more as he fell on it with all his weight.

Jumping to his feet, McRae stood waiting for Nelson to

get up. But the damaged leg was causing the big man agony. Rolling on to his stomach, he managed to push himself upright, although standing with great difficulty on one leg.

Remembering the advantage taken of an accidental collision with a pony on the night at the corral, McRae showed no mercy. Stepping in close to Nelson, he hammered his body with damaging punches, before switching his attack to the head. Driven backwards, denied any support by his damaged leg, Reuben Nelson's efforts to fight back were big-fisted punches that were either easily evaded or taken without flinching by McRae. He felt and heard a cheekbone crack under his knuckles.

The beginning of the end came for Nelson when he was backed against a tree. If ever McRae had seen stark, naked fear in a human face, it stared at him out of that of the man in front of him. His broken nose bled profusely, and his right eye was swollen grotesquely. Unable to slide to the ground, his face was battered to a pulp until McRae, out of compassion rather then fatigue, stepped back.

Shaken by having viewed the violent attack, Sanchez dropped to his knees beside Nelson to administer what aid he could. Uneasy at being unarmed, McRae turned with the intention of retrieving his gunbelt from the branch, to find Dean Razzo standing between him and the tree.

Thumbs hooked in his gunbelt, a sneer on his brutish face, Razzo said. 'I reckon what you've done to Reuben is going to make Max Nelson as mad as a peeled rattler, McRae.'

'Reuben had it coming,' McRae opined looking over to where Sanchez had propped a disfigured Nelson into a sitting position. Coming back to Razzo, he said. 'Stand aside.'

Shaking his head, Razzo refused. 'I reckon as how you can't have your gun back. We wus going to run you outta the valley, mister. But now you've gone and done this to Reub, I don't see you going anywheres.'

'Dean,' Sanchez called, as he propped a seated Reuben against the tree. Walking over, he took care not to come between Razzo and McRae. 'We can't allow Max to see his boy in this state.'

'We won't,' Razzo informed him. 'We'll take him down to the line camp and fix him up, once I've dealt with our pardner here.'

'What you gonna do with him, Dean?'

'Well,' Razzo mused, 'he sure as hell won't be needing that pony of his to ride away from here.'

A worried expression on his face, Sanchez warned. 'Max wants McRae, Dean. He needs him to finish up what we started. He ain't likely to thank us for getting shot of him.'

'McRae's a renegade, Sanchez. Max'll just figure that he's lit out on him,' Razzo explained, then called to Nelson. 'Can you get yourself up and come over here, Reub?'

It took Nelson much effort and time to get upright, and he needed to rest before taking the short walk. His left eye was completely closed, his nose had been knocked sideways, and the broken side of his face was badly out of shape.

After briefly studying him, Razzo commented. 'You do'n look so bad, Reub.'

'Land Sakes!' Sanchez vehemently disagreed. 'He looks like he's been rowed up Salt River.'

'We'll tell Max his bronc throw'd him, Sanchez. Now, give Reub your gun.'

Not understanding what was happening, Sanchez hesitated before handing his gun to an equally bewildered Nelson. Then Razzo spoke to McRae, and they understood.

'I'm going to step aside, McRae, so's you can fetch your gunbelt. By my figuring it ain't an almighty distance from you, no more than fifteen feet. The snag is, Reuben probably do'n feel right kindly toward you, and dang me if Sanchez ain't dun gone and give him a gun. But I do'n see how that will worry a fast moving hombre like you.'

McRae accepted that he was facing impossible odds. Reuben Nelson appeared to be sufficiently recovered to be able to gun him down before he could reach the tree. If Nelson was too feeble, or if he missed, McRae was in no doubt that Razzo, who couldn't risk him getting his gun, would draw and shoot him down in cold blood. Nevertheless, he saw the only other option was to die where he was now standing.

He quickly formed a plan that he recognized was barely workable. Nelson, obviously not a fast thinker, would be expecting him to make a dash for his own gun. If he ran at Nelson instead of the tree, there was a chance of him getting Sanchez's gun. It was a scheme that depended on Razzo holding fire for fear of hitting Nelson. Another disadvantage was the distance between him and Nelson being roughly that as between him and the tree. If Dean Razzo was the capable gunfighter he judged him to be, then McRae believed that his change of course would fool him only for a split second.

Aware that he had no alternative but to run the risk, he was about to leap into action when he sensed that a change had come over the other men. Then he realized what had brought it about. A rider had come down through a little gully that led into the flat and was now loping through the long saccatone grass, heading for the foot of the hill on which McRae and the others stood. The distance was too great to identify the rider. The likelihood of it being a Nelson man warned McRae to remain still and not take any chances. The possibility that it might not be a *Two Circles* man had Razzo and his companions stay their hand.

Coming steadily on, the rider topped the crest of the hill. It was Juanita Nelson, looking every inch a Mexican lady on her Appaloosa horse. Her appearance dismayed all four men. The fact that neither Reuben Nelson, Sanchez nor Razzo knew what effect her arrival would have on the life and death drama she had ridden into had them stand uncomfortably around. Though none of the three, including her son, had any respect for Juanita, she was the boss's wife. That gave her power over them.

Also unable to predict what the next few minutes would bring, McRae welcomed the fact that it had provided him with a reprieve, although it might well be of short duration. He watched the woman carefully, trying to discover from her movements what she had in mind.

She rode closer, her face expressionless. Keeping all four men guessing, she guided her horse round them slowly and elegantly in a tight arc. Leaning over sideways in the saddle, she reached out to deftly lift McRae's belt from the tree. Completing a circle, she handed the belt to him, remarking. 'Who would believe that Maury McRae could be so careless.'

Thankfully taking the belt, he buckled it on then took out the six-shooter, rolled the cylinder, then returned the gun to its holster. His relief at apparently having Juanita on his side was equalled by the consternation of Razzo,

Reuben Nelson and Sanchez. All four men were left in limbo once more, wondering what was about to happen as Juanita gracefully dismounted and hitched her pony beside McRae's. Though Max Nelson was very much his own man, his second wife influenced him more than he realized. All three *Two Circles* men were conscious of the trouble she could make for them.

Joe Fielding, a callow youth in a land of rugged men, nervously entered the sheriffs office and put the letter on the desk in front of Fernando Wood. As a relative newcomer to the West, Fielding stood waiting timidly, afraid of tough Westerners such as the sheriff, scared to speak for fear of making a fool of himself, and desperately anxious to leave and return to the familiarity of the ranch.

Taking the folded paper up without opening it, Wood leaned back in his chair, his cold eyes assessing the youngster standing nervously in front of him. He asked, more harshly than he had intended, 'Who might you be, son?'

'Joe Fielding, sir,' the boy stammered. 'I works out at the *Double U*.'

'Ernie Roderick, eh? Well, kid, you could do a whole heap worse than work for Ernie. I figure this letter's from him?'

'Yes, sir.'

Favouring his left hand while cautiously concealing a swollen right wrist under the sleeve of his coat as he unfolded the letter, Fernando Wood was an unhappy man. Less than an hour ago he had received the bad news from Dr Faylen when visiting his surgery. He had gone to the doctor after weeks of first trying to ignore a wrist that was gradually becoming more and more misshapen, painful and inflexible, followed by having to accept that something could be seriously wrong. Even then it had taken him three days to force himself to consult the doctor. Always having been superbly fit, it seemed that it was letting himself down to admit to a physical defect.

'What is it, Doc?' he had enquired, hoping for a reassuring answer that it was a trivial, passing ailment.

'I'm pretty sure it's arthritis, Fernando,' Faylen, his face serious, had replied.

'How long will that take to clear up?'

In the knowledge of what affect an exact diagnosis would have on the sheriff, the doctor had delayed answering. Then his reply had shocked Wood. 'Arthritis, a common, progressive illness, is incurable.'

'Can you suggest anything, Doc?' the sheriff had asked, adding, 'As long as it's not that I should practise until I have perfected a fast left-hand draw.'

'I can give you something to ease the pain, and advise you on heat treatment that you can apply,' the doctor had replied. Quiet in thought for a moment or two, he then said. 'I am aware that you could be put at great risk if this disability became known. No one will learn about it from me, Fernando. It is plain that you can no longer continue in your profession, and I would urge you to consider retiring without delay.'

'I'm too young to retire, Doc.'

'You're too young to die, Fernando.'

'Maybe so,' Wood had acknowledged. 'I suppose that there would be plenty ready to hit the vengeance trail if they learned I was no longer a fast gun. But I've never run away from anything. Doc, and I don't see myself doing so now.'

'I'm not suggesting that you run. But i would advise that

you quietly relinquish your position as sheriff.'

Though he had thanked Dr Faylen for his kind advice, Wood had no intention of taking it. He left the surgery determined to find a way to carry on. Enforcing the law without fear or favour was his life. There was no way that he could let go of the position as sheriff that he cherished.

Yet now, before reading the letter that he held, knowing that it was a request for help, he saw starkly and for the first time, the virtual impossibility of carrying out his duties as a lawman with a gun hand that daily became less flexible. Comprehension of this made him despondent.

Neither did the situation described by Roderick, an honest, uncomplicated man, seem credible. Nothing he was reading fitted in with his knowledge of the people involved. It was probably a vain hope, but he decided to discover if the boy who had bought the letter had any answers.

Raising his head to look at Fielding, he asked. 'Is Pete Goodson still alive?'

'Yes. They do say that the bullet hit him in the leg.'

'And it was Maury McRae who shot him?'

'That's what Zec Cordell told Mr Roderick, sir,' Fielding replied without committing himself.

It didn't add up. Wood couldn't think of any rational way that the clumsy *Double U* straw boss could be transformed into a gunfighter. Anyway, if that transformation had miraculously occurred and Goodson had faced up to McRae, then he would have taken a bullet in his heart, not his leg. A man like McRae would never miss his target.

Taking time out for some deep thinking, Wood then spoke to an apprehensive Fielding. 'I want you to listen real good, son, and take this message back to your boss, word for word. Do you think you can do that?'

'I'll try real hard, sir.'

'I'm sure that you will, son. I want you to tell Ernie Roderick that I'll be out there in the valley as soon as I possibly can. Explain to him that Judge Baldwin arrives in town tonight, and the court starts up tomorrow. I expect court to run for two days. Once it is over, I'll be heading for Cottonwood Valley straight away. Have you got that, Joe?'

'I sure have, sir,' a smiling Fielding confirmed, made to feel important by the sheriff's use of his first name.

'Then off you go, and good luck.'

When the boy had gone out of the door, Wood opened and closed the fingers of his right hand repeatedly. Then he manipulated his wrist. The pain didn't distress him as much as the rigidity of the joint. He wondered how much worse it would be in two day's time when he headed for the *Double U* ranch.

If things in the valley developed along the gunsmoke-shrouded lines he anticipated, of what use would be a lawman who had difficulty drawing his gun, let alone firing it effectively? No one must know, and it worried him what Heather Cordell might think of him if he shirked his duty. Was it possible that she might judge him to be a coward?

Having always been a self-confident, proud fighting man, he felt diminished by the reduction of movement in his gun hand. He had to adapt to the knowledge that life would never again be the same as it was. What he could not accept was that Sheriff Fernando Wood would never again be the man that he was.

'What now, McRae?' Juanita asked, her Spanish accent

more noticeable than McRae remembered.

She leaned lazily against a rock as she spoke, but McRae was certain that she was far from relaxed. 'You have a choice to make. The situation is that you are only up against one man. You've beaten Reuben until he looks even uglier than usual, and he wouldn't have the guts to face you if you hadn't. Sanchez doesn't count. He's just a buckaroo, a good bush roper, maybe, but when it comes to guns he couldn't hit a bull's ass with a handful of banjos. So it comes down to being between you and Razzo.'

Aware that she was sanctioning him challenging Razzo, probably even urging him to do so, McRae looked to where the bowler-hatted man stood, obviously undecided as to what he should do. Getting involved in a gunfight at that time did not fit in with the plans McRae had provisionally made.

'All I'm looking to do is my job,' Razzo said after a considerable amount of thinking time. 'That's ranch work, not gunplay.'

Since first meeting him, McRae had regarded Razzo as a former gunfighter, whose self-assured attitude stemmed from confidence in his own skill with a gun. Right now, McRae concluded, Razzo was not in the least unnerved by the thought of facing him. His reticence came from not wanting to alienate Max Nelson.

'That's not the way it looked when I got here,' Juanita commented cynically. 'The way that I see it, you three were about to do McRae real harm. With that in mind, McRae now has the opportunity to make all three of you pay for that. I personally hope that he does.'

Waiting for McRae's reaction to what she had said, she watched him intently. Instinctively craving vengeance, he reminded himself that it would be a pleasure that he couldn't afford. Certain that he could beat Dean Razzo to the draw, he was keenly aware of the consequence of doing so. Max Nelson probably needed him badly enough to overlook the fact that he had smashed his son so seriously that his face, now a swollen mass of bruises and cuts, was unrecognizable, his body so badly hammered that he winced with pain with every small movement, and he was lame. But the rancher was unlikely to welcome the news that he had killed Razzo. Blood was said to be thicker than water, but the capable Razzo was by far more useful to Max Nelson than Reuben was.

'I'll leave it for now, ma'am,' McRae said, obviously disappointing her.

'Then you can ride back with me, McRae, and I will make certain that my husband knows that his son brought upon himself the misfortune he suffered at your hands.'

Walking beside her to where their horses were tethered, McRae had no wish to hide behind Juanita. Yet it was to his advantage to have her smooth things over with Max Nelson. With a bit of luck, his scheme would work, and he would soon be leaving the valley and escaping from the bounty hunter who had dogged his trail for so long.

As Juanita and McRae rode away side by side, she asked him. 'Aren't you nervous turning your back on them?'

'If any of the three should make a move, I'll know about it before they can pull the trigger.'

'I should have known that,' she chided herself gently, and spoke no more until they were nearing the ranch. What she said then came as a surprise to McRae.

'What if we kept riding?' Juanita mused, slowing her horse. 'If we went on until we rode into another world. Entered into a new life?'

127

'I guess we'd find the world was about the same as this one, and our pasts would catch up with us before we could enjoy the new life.'

Despite being made unhappy by his dispiriting answer, she looked at him wistfully as they dismounted outside the ranch house.

NINE

Coming into the cabin for breakfast after completing his early-morning chores, Zec Cordell asked. 'How is he this morning?'

'Ssshh,' his sister cautioned, placing one finger against her lips. 'He's sleeping.'

'Good,' Zec said quietly as he pulled out a chair to sit at the table. He rubbed his hands in glee as Heather put a plate of fried food in front of him.

Sitting down opposite to him, elbows on the table, head resting on her hands, her brow creased by worry, she said. 'Have we done wrong, Zec?'

'By sending for Fernando?' he queried as he ate ravenously. 'I don't think so.'

Their problem had begun the previous afternoon when Pete Goodson, now recovering fast, had been well enough to talk. Hoping against hope that the answer would be 'no' now that he had regained full consciousness, she asked if it was definitely Maury McRae who had shot him. Vigorously nodding an affirmative, Goodson had shattered her, but she had experienced immense relief when he had explained that it was he who had confronted McRae and not the other way around.

'I must have been real loco,' Goodson had told her and Zec ruefully. 'I met him by chance close to the *Double U.* Certain that he was up to no good snooping around there, I challenged him. I wasn't skeered, but I should have been. What chance would a plug-ugly like me have against a man like McRae?'

'Did he take up the challenge?' Zec had asked.

'I didn't give him no chance not to. I pushed him and pushed him, and I went for my gun first. I didn't so much as clear leather when he fired. He spared my life on purpose.'

'But he left you to die,' Zec pointed out.

'No, that isn't true. McRae tied a—'

As Goodson had searched for the word he needed, Heather had interrupted. 'He used his bandanna to tie a tourniquet round your leg.'

'That's right, Heather.'

Zec had been puzzled. 'But how did you manage to come to us?'

'McRae brought me here.'

Pouring her brother another cup of coffee at the breakfast table, Heather expressed her concerns. 'We've sent for Fernando, but it looks as if we are wrong. McRae couldn't be doing Max Nelson's dirty work if he took care of Pete in that way.'

'We can't be sure of that,' Zec cautioned. 'Pete came upon him poking around near Ernie's place. What reason would he have to be there if he wasn't acting for Nelson?'

Not having an answer to her brother's question, Heather remained silent. But her thoughts were busy with pushing the stubbornly remaining last bit of doubt about Maury McRae from her mind.

Max Nelson was seething with anger when he walked up to where McRae was grooming his pony. Though McRae accepted the injuries he had inflicted on Reuben Nelson was the cause of much of the anger, the extreme agitation that was so noticeable in Nelson convinced him that the rancher had other problems of a much greater magnitude.

'You went against my orders, McRae. I said I'd deal with my boy, and being a man of my word I would have done so.'

'I got kinda tired of waiting, I guess, Mr Nelson,' McRae explained. 'When the opportunity turned up, it was just too good to ignore.'

'That's not the sort of behaviour I expect from those on my payroll.'

'So you want me out of here?'

'Not at all,' Nelson hastily assured him. 'You've earned your money since you've been here, and tomorrow you'll earn it big-time. Me, you, Dean Razzo, and Reuben will be riding to the Cordells' place. That Zec Cordell has robbed me of some of my best beef, and now it's payback time. Come candle-lighting time tomorrow, I want him and that sister of his out of Cottonwood Valley for good. Have you got any problem with that, McRae?'

McRae shrugged. 'None at all. Fixing these rustlers is what you hired me for, Mr Nelson. What about Ernie Roderick?'

'We'll ride out to his place straight after. Roderick has a family, and he won't want to risk anything happening to them once we tell him what we did at the Cordells' homestead.'

'I guess you got it all figured out right and proper, Mr Nelson.'

131

McRae's compliment brought a fleeting smile to Nelson's face. 'That's the way it is, McRae. I do the thinking, and you do the shooting.'

'That's the way I like it,' McRae responded.

'Good,' Nelson said with a satisfied nod as he turned to walk away. Then he paused for a moment to ask. 'You got any problem with riding beside Reuben tomorrow, McRae?'

'None at all, Mr Nelson,' McRae promised. 'As far as I'm concerned that's all settled and done with.'

Remaining seated at the table after dinner, when Zec and Pete Goodson, the latter hobbling along with the aid of a stick, had gone out to do some work, Sheriff Wood answered Heather's question.

'I came straight out here to have you and Zec tell me what the latest situation is. I'll be riding back into Gray's Flat later. Durell is still there, and I need to put my ear to the ground, so to speak, so as I know what Max Nelson has in mind. Martha Tinkler has asked me to attend the inaugural meeting of the town council tomorrow evening, and I can probably learn a lot there. But I'll not be far away from you, Zec, and the Rodericks at any time.'

'I'm glad that you're here, Fernando,' a grateful Heather said. 'Do you think it possible that Maury McRae will help Nelson move against us?'

'That's a difficult question to answer, Heather. McRae isn't the kind of renegade that I detest, but there are side issues to consider. For instance, Max Nelson desperately wants you, Zec, and the Rodericks out of the valley. I know that for a fact. McRae is certain to be short of money, having had Durell on his tail for so long. He needs to get away from Durell, and that isn't easy when he's stony broke and the bounty hunter leaves him no opportunity to commit a robbery. Nelson needs a fast gun like McRae, so he'll be ready to pay dear for his services. Every man is said to have price.'

'I know that saying, but I can't believe that it could apply to a man like Maury McRae.'

Though it was distressful to hear Heather so stoutly defend another man, Wood was above the low-grade emotion of jealousy. He advised kindly, 'Dire circumstances can have the best of us sacrifice our principles, Heather. And I would say that right now McRae's circumstances are about as dire as they come.'

'I understand,' Heather said gloomily. Then she tried to brighten up by pointing to a plate and asking the sheriff. 'Would you like another of my cookies?'

'I shouldn't, but they are really good,' Wood said boyishly as he stretched out his right hand to the plate. He realized his mistake too late. The sleeve of his coat had ridden up, putting his swollen wrist on display.

With a gasp of concern, Heather lightly grasped his forearm. 'What on earth have you done to your wrist, Fernando?'

'Doc Faylen says it's arthritis.' Wood had no option but to answer her.

'I don't know—' Heather deliberated as she examined the swollen joint. 'I wouldn't doubt Dr Faylen, but it could be just sprained. Have you had a fall, or hurt your wrist in some other way?'

'Not that I remember, but I do lead a pretty active life, Heather.'

'That's the trouble with you tough guys,' Heather reproached him, smiling fondly as she did so. 'You're too stupid to notice pain.'

'Maybe, but I sure notice this pain in my wrist. Do you think it is arthritis, Heather?'

'I'm not a qualified doctor.'

'I have total faith in you,' Wood declared.

Holding her bottom lip with her teeth, leaving marks, as she turned his wrist this way and that. She asked. 'Did Dr Faylen offer any treatment?'

'He gave me some pills, and told me to heat up a flannel and wrap it round my wrist'

'I think your wrist is sprained. Have you got a couple of hours before you have to leave for Gray's Flat?'

'I'm in no hurry. Are you going to fix my wrist?'

'I'll warn you first, then it's up to you whether you accept, Fernando. This isn't exactly kill or cure, but if Dr Faylen is right and I am wrong, then my treatment will probably do more harm than good.'

'I'll go along with you, Heather.'

Soaking a square of towelling in cold water, Heather wrapped it round his swollen wrist, then bandaged it tightly. She told him. 'This is the start of the treatment. We leave that in place for twenty minutes, then take it off and expose the wrist to the air for twenty minutes before repeating the cold cloth and bandaging for another twenty minutes, and so on. Keep your right arm high, above the level of your heart, for as long as possible to drain any blood impurities from your wrist. This treatment should be continued for twenty-four hours. Where will you be staying tonight?'

'At Miss Tinkler's place.'

'Well, you take the cloth and bandage with you, and carry on the treatment for as long as you can. You'll find it awkward to bandage your wrist with the other hand, but you'll soon get the hang of it.'

'I'm obliged to you, Heather,' Wood said, and all the feeling he had for her was in his eyes.

A little embarrassed by this, she said severely, 'If this does bring the swelling down and eases the pain, don't even think of drawing your gun with that hand for at least a week, perhaps two weeks. Do I have your word on that?'

'You know best, Heather,' he said, avoiding giving his word, but implying that he would obey her instructions. Then he made an earnest plea. 'You'll keep this problem with my gun hand just between you and me?'

'Of course,' she replied, aware of what a harrowing difficulty the injured wrist must be for a man whose life depended on the ability to draw a gun fast.

'What's the kerosene for, Mr Nelson?'

McRae asked the question when he saw Reuben pouring kerosene into a small barrel while they were getting ready to ride away from the ranch He heard Dean Razzo give a short derisory laugh, apparently at the naivety of the question. The elaborate preparations being made, with what he judged to be an overemphasis on guns and ammunition, made him uneasy. The inclusion of a flammable liquid increased his fears.

It seemed to McRae that Max Nelson didn't intend to give him an answer. But, after fastening the saddle cinch under his horse, he straightened up, head back looking up at the sky as he spoke, 'Can you think of any reason why I would have need of a homesteader's shack on my land, McRae.'

'No, I don't say as I can.'

McRae knew the full meaning of what Nelson had said before he'd given his reply. However, though chilled to the core by what the rancher intended, he had to go along with it.

'It ain't the Fourth of July,' Reuben chuckled, 'but it will sure look like it.'

'Not so much of this, Reuben,' his father ordered, making a symbolic mouth opening and closing with the thumb and forefinger of one hand. 'Get on with what you have to do.'

'Let the boy have his fun, Max,' a grinning Dean Razzo advised. 'I'm looking to see how McRae handles himself when the chips are down. Could be we'll see he's not what he's cracked up to be.'

'You could find that out right now, Razzo,' McRae offered in a deceptively moderate tone.

'Now that,' Razzo sneered, doing a quarter turn to face McRae squarely, 'would suit me right fine. I'm ready, McRae, so make your play any time to suit you.'

Welcoming the diversion, pleased by the thought that by killing Razzo he would be taking out one of the biggest threats against the Cordells, McRae took a sack of Bull Durham from his shirt pocket and casually rolled a cigarette, saying, 'You're making it too easy for me, Razzo. You go for your gun first.'

Anger reddening his face, Razzo was poised for a speedy draw when Max Nelson stepped between him and McRae.

'Hold it right there, you pair of danged fools,' the rancher shouted. 'I don't give a darn if you blow each other to kingdom come, but not before you've done what I'm paying you to do. Both of you get back to what you were doing. We're moving out in half an hour.'

With the moment that had held so much promise gone, McRae walked over to the smithy to collect his slicker. Thunderclouds had been gathering from the west all through that dark day, and a deep grumbling could be

136

heard from beyond the horizon.

With the rolled up slicker under his arm, he was coming down the outside staircase when he became aware of a slight movement in the passageway between the smithy and a feed store. Leaping lightly down the last two steps, he pulled his back in tight against the wall, ready for whatever threat it was.

Then there came another movement. This time he saw that it was Juanita, holding up a hand to signal that she knew he was there, while at the same time peeping out of the passageway to check on her husband, his son, and Razzo. Satisfied that they couldn't see her, she crossed the passageway to stand beside McRae.

'What is going to happen?' she asked fearfully.

McRae shrugged. 'He hasn't told me his plans, Juanita.'

'Whatever he intends to do, innocent people are going to get hurt, aren't they?'

'I guess that's so,' McRae acknowledged.

'You could stop it happening, Maury.'

'I'm on the run, running for my life,' McRae explained. 'All I can do is follow Nelson's orders, collect the money that he owes me, and ride away before either the sheriff or the bounty hunter puts an end to my life.'

'But—' Juanita stopped speaking as her husband shouted for McRae.

'McRae!'

'I have to go,' McRae told her.

She caught hold of his arm, her fingers digging in. 'You are a good man, Maury McRae. I will pray for you. *Vaya con Dios.*'

Prising her fingers from his arm, he walked away to join Max Nelson and the others.

*

It was late afternoon at the Cordell homestead, and all was peaceful. Heather was seated in a chair, a sewing basket on her lap as she industriously plied a needle and thread to a strip of striped material. Occasionally, she glanced from the corners of her eyes to where her brother was hunkered, cleaning a rifle. They needed to be prepared, she accepted that. Even so, awareness of Zec getting the rifle ready robbed what could have been a grand afternoon of all its pleasures.

Pete Goodson was standing at the window, resting the knee of his injured leg on a chair for support. Earlier he had been talking of returning to the *Double U*. All three of them had positively discussed the prospect of him doing so. All three of them had secretly and dismally wondered if there would be a ranch and an Ernie Roderick to return to when the time came.

'Riders heading this way,' Goodson tersely announced.

Placing her sewing on the floor beside the chair, Heather sprang to her feet, running to the window. Zec came up to stand behind her, and the metallic clicking sound of him loading the rifle chilled her to the bone. Looking out at scenery she had come to love, but at that moment had become a desolate, silent world, she had to squint against a lowering sun. Then she saw five horsemen riding abreast down the slight gradient that swept towards the cabin from the base of a hill.

The riders approached at a steady pace that was all the more frightening for her because it emphasised their sense of purpose. Goodson identified them in a hushed voice. 'That's Max Nelson in the middle, with Reuben and Razzo on his left, and Sanchez and McRae riding on his right.'

Hearing McRae named as one of the riders moved

Heather close to tears. Her hopes that he would not find it possible to act against her and Zec were cruelly dashed. She tried to reason that it made little difference. Even if McRae wasn't there, her brother would be no match for the menacing Dean Razzo. Her brother saying that he was going out to meet the *Two Circles* men suddenly distracted her thoughts. Zec was taking his rifle with him, and the consequences of such an action terrified her.

'Zec,' she cried as he headed for the door. 'If you must go out there, then leave your rifle here.'

With an emphatic shake of his head, he told her. 'No. I have to let them see that I mean business.'

'The fact that there is just one of you against five isn't likely to impress them,' she argued frantically.

'Heather is right, Zec,' Goodson said to support her.

But it made no difference. Always headstrong, Zec went out of the door, with a very frightened Heather and a lame Goodson following close behind.

Reining their horses to a stop a few yards from them, the five riders sat unspeaking. Max Nelson took off his Stetson and beat it against an elbow to remove the dust of a long ride. Putting the hat back on, he pointed at the rifle that Zec was holding at the ready.

'Don't make things worse for you and your sister, Cordell. Put that weapon down and we'll talk like rational human beings.'

'There's nothing for us to talk about, Nelson.'

Anger raised Max Nelson's voice by at least one octave. 'That's where you're wrong, badly wrong, son. I've got a whole heap to say, beginning with the fact that you have stolen the last cattle that you'll ever steal from me. McRae here has been working for me for some time, tracking you and Roderick. He's found irrefutable evidence that you and that two-bit rancher are responsible for the theft of every one of the stock taken from me in the last year or so.'

Hearing this wiped from Heather's mind the last vain hope that McRae had not become a Nelson man. Pete Goodson had been right about the reason why McRae had been snooping around Ernie Roderick's ranch. She was both upset and worried, and became more frightened as she heard her brother argue.

'I've stolen nary a one of your beef, Nelson, and you know it,' Zec Cordell retorted. 'If you believe otherwise, then I suggest that you produce whatever evidence you have to Sheriff Wood.'

'That won't be necessary, Cordell. The proof that I have is so strong that I intend to take action first and show the evidence to Fernando Wood afterwards. Before the sun drops below' – he stopped talking to turn in the saddle and to stretch out an arm and point at the remote mountain range behind him – 'them peaks, I want you and Miss Cordell out of Cottonwood Valley.'

Keeping his eyes on Max Nelson, Zec asked McRae, 'Is it right that you've got evidence against me and Ernie, McRae?'

'It's right, Cordell.'

'Well, I don't believe either you or Nelson. And I certainly ain't going to move off my place, even if there's ten of you ride up to drive me out.'

'Tell him to lay that rifle down, Razzo,' Nelson ordered.

Making a show of placing a hand on the butt of his holstered gun, Razzo said in a threatening tone, 'Take a look at what you're up against and see sense, Cordell.'

Trying to think of some way, some effective appeal she could make to her brother, Heather saw Pete Goodson

limp forward until he was between Zec and the five *Two
Circles* men, with his back to them. He held out a hand,
and she heard him say. 'We'll work this out somehow, Zec.
But give me the rifle now. You don't want to put Heather
at risk.'

To Heather's surprise and delight, this plea had her
brother pass his rifle to Goodson, who walked to place it
against the wheel of their buckboard.

'That's better,' Max Nelson commented, a smirk of
satisfaction on his face as he addressed the now unarmed
Zec. 'Now listen up, Cordell. You are finished here. We're
going to burn this shack of yours to the ground, but even
though you are nothing but a goddam rustler, I am a fair
man. So you and Miss Cordell have five minutes to pack
your belongings. Then you are free to ride out of this
valley. No one will stop you, no attempt will be made to do
harm to either of you, unless you should be foolish
enough to try to come back into Cottonwood Valley, today
or any other day. Get the kerosene, Reuben, and give
those ramshackle walls a good soaking.'

'NO.'

Her brother's shout of protest startled Heather. She saw
Reuben Nelson twist in the saddle to unstrap a cask that
she assumed contained the kerosene his father had
referred to. The unreality of what was happening
disorientated her. She tried to regain normality by looking
around at familiar scenery. But the silent hills, the sun
retiring for the day above the mountain peaks, and the
great, vast arc of sky that yawned above her also seemed
unreal. It was as though she had been suddenly thrust into
a land of terrifying fantasy.

It was the sight of McRae moving his pony slowly
forward that jolted her at least partially back into ordinary

conscious. He rode past where she, her brother, and Goodson stood. When he was behind them he turned his pony, dismounted, and walked up to stand beside Zec.

Mystified, Max and Reuben Nelson, Razzo, and Sanchez had silently watched this manoeuvre by McRae. Now they all exchanged puzzled glances. At last Max Nelson recovered sufficiently to enquire. 'What are you doing, McRae?'

'Repaying a debt, I guess. Miss Cordell saved my life a few weeks back.'

'What about the debt you owe me. I hired you to track down those rustling my cattle.'

'You haven't paid me yet, Nelson, so I owe you nothing.'

'But I need you to attest the evidence, to tell Sheriff Wood what you witnessed.'

'I'm willing to do that,' McRae told him reassuringly. 'I can swear to the sheriff that you rustled your own cattle, and led false trails so as to incriminate Zec Cordell and Ernie Roderick.'

'Have you gone plumb loco?' Max Nelson shouted.

Glancing at Razzo, he must have conveyed some kind of command. Razzo went for his gun. His movements were sure and startlingly fast, but McRae was quicker. He had drawn and squeezed the trigger in a lightning blur. Dean Razzo, not having triggered his gun, sat motionless in the saddle. A dark hole that oozed thick blood had appeared between his wide-open, staring eyes.

Ears ringing from the sound of McRae's gun, a horrified Heather watched Razzo slowly fall backwards over the rump of his horse. Both feet trapped in the stirrups, Razzo's body hung off the back of the horse, his head dangling some three feet above the ground. This gruesome sight took on a new dreadfulness as the horse, driven crazy by the weight of the dead body dragging behind it, ran amok.

Shrieking horrifically, the animal reared time after time, then swung from side to side in attempts at freeing itself of the burden. Head down, it kicked repeatedly with its rear legs, its hoofs pounding Razzo's body. Shocked into immobility, the two Nelsons and Sanchez sat helplessly in the saddle.

Heather turned away, covering her eyes with her hands, but the sound of pounding hoofs forced her to look. Razzo's horse was running in ragged circles, still screaming in fear. It circled close to the corral posts, and on the next lap crashed into them. In pain as the sharp edge of a snapped-off post jabbed into its flank, the animal did a twisting turn on the spot, cracking Razzo's head against the corral with a sound as loud as a gunshot.

Then it charged away from the traumatized spectators. About twenty yards along the trail on which Nelson and the others had arrived, the body at last broke free and crashed to the ground. Relieved, the horse stood, convulsing so hard that its shaking was clearly visible from a distance.

Without a word, the Nelsons and Sanchez wheeled their horses about and rode away. Reaching where Razzo lay, they dismounted. Heather, Zec and Goodson watched Sanchez hold the reins of Razzo's horse, calming it while the Nelsons draped the body over its back and secured it. Then they mounted and rode away, with Sanchez holding the reins of Razzo's horse.

'They'll be heading for Ernie's place,' Zec predicted, his voice made shaky by the terrible scene just witnessed.

'How can we warn him?' Goodson enquired.

'No need,' McRae advised. 'Nelson can do nothing without Razzo. I guess he's beaten.'

Thanks to you, Heather said gratefully inside her head.

TEN

It had been difficult when Max Nelson and his son and stepson had ridden away the previous afternoon. McRae's rapid change of sides had left the Cordells confused. He had explained that he had gone along with Nelson only until it was likely they would be caused harm.

On entering the cabin next morning, McRae found Heather, Zec, and Goodson at the breakfast table. The prospect of trouble to come had created a tense atmosphere. Heather immediately sprang to her feet, saying, 'Take a seat, Maury. I'll get your breakfast.' Then she asked him, 'Do you think Max Nelson will be back?'

Pulling a chair up to the table, McRae answered her. 'I reckon not. Without Dean Razzo, he doesn't now have the power to drive you and Roderick out.'

'Reuben's mighty handy with a gun,' Pete Goodson pointed out.

'When tin cans are the target,' McRae agreed. 'He lacks what it takes to be a gunfighter.'

'How do you see this ending, Maury?' Heather asked, placing his breakfast on the table.

'I wouldn't like to take a guess,' McRae admitted. 'But I'll be here with you and Zec until it's over. I reckon this is what I need to have me stop running and settle the Durell thing.'

'Your last trail,' Heather sighed, puzzling her brother and Goodson, but not McRae.

Glancing out of the window Zec warned his sister, 'You'd better get back to the stove, Heather. Fernando is riding up on us bright and early.'

'Would you care to take breakfast, Mr Nelson?'

Until Martha Tinkler asked the question as she brought Durell his breakfast, Max Nelson had not noticed how ravenous he was. Leaving *Two Circles* before sunup, he had been relieved to find Durell alone in the dining room. He said, 'That's very kind of you, Miss Tinkler.'

'Add it to my bill, Miss Tinker,' Dwell said cordially, then spoke quietly to Nelson. 'Losing both McRae and Razzo was a blow. What you need is a change of strategy.'

'I'm afraid that I don't understand.'

Taking time out to slice up the food on his plate before laying the knife aside, Durell forked food into his mouth. While chewing, he explained, 'You are meeting the railroad agents on Monday, so you have no time to hire replacement gunfighters. I would suggest a political solution. I can manipulate Miss Tinkler to do what we want with the new town council.'

'Which is?' a keenly interested Nelson enquired.

'We have agreed that we should have six councillors. She hasn't an inkling that I plan to choose eleven candidates of weak character, men easy to influence. You will be the twelfth candidate, and I will propose that as a fine, upstanding local rancher, you be elected as mayor. My spell as a congressman was an apprenticeship in falsehood. In my experience, the general public almost volunteer to be fooled. I will conduct the meeting, and your first act as mayor will be to appoint me as town marshal. As town marshal, I can deal with Sheriff Wood then McRae under the law.'

Nelson asked. 'With respect, are you confident of beating both of them to the draw?'

With short laugh, Durell replied, 'Don't doubt it for one moment, Nelson. I will remove Wood and McRae, the only obstacles on your path to the sole ownership of Cottonwood Valley.'

'I will still have no way of removing the Cordells and the Rodericks by Monday.'

'With me to act for you, you have,' Durell said.

'But why would you side with me?'

'You are already a wealthy man, Nelson, and you'll be a whole lot richer when the railroad deal is finalized. It will be fair to share that prosperity with me, for services rendered.'

Though desperate to reject this proposal, Nelson could see no way to do so. He was overwhelmed by the knowledge that he had relinquished control of his Cottonwood Valley plans.

'I agree with McRae that Max Nelson is no longer a threat to you and Zec,' Sheriff Wood advised Heather as she walked with him to his horse.

The Cordells had reported yesterday's dramatic incident to the sheriff. Having expressed his regret and apologized for not being there for them at so crucial a time, and being satisfied that Max Nelson was no longer a threat to Heather and her brother, he was returning to Gray's Flat.

His face wore an expression of concern. 'You seem to

be greatly troubled, Heather.'

'I suppose that I have got into the habit of worrying, Fernando,' she said ashamedly. 'Maury believes that we should all go to the town council meeting this evening.'

'I agree with him. Martha Tinkler is the force behind the forming of a council, and she will see to it that the right type of candidate is chosen for election. Now that Nelson's big plans have been thwarted, a town council will hold the power here.'

'But that man Durell is still in town, and I don't think it wise for Maury to take the risk.'

This made the sheriff uncomfortable, and he looked around him as if hoping to pick the right words from the surroundings before speaking. When he did manage to say something, it was to ask bashfully. 'May I speak freely, Heather?'

'Of course you may.'

'I think that McRae would like to start a new life, and he can't do that until he frees himself from his unfortunate past. To that end, he would seem determined to face Durell. Hopefully, the outcome will favour McRae, and I would like to assure you that I will have the wanted notice cancelled.'

'Assure me?' Heather, not understanding, queried. Then what Wood had said suddenly registered with her. With an incredulous gasp, she said. 'You think that he is doing this for me?'

The sheriff nodded. 'That's obvious, and I had the impression that is what you want.'

'Oh, no. Maury is basically a good man, but whatever happens, I could neither forget nor live with the knowledge of what he once was, Fernando.' Disturbed by what Wood had suggested, Heather quickly changed the subject. Reaching out for his right hand, she asked. 'How is your wrist?'

'I've followed your advice, and the swelling has gone right down.'

'Is there much pain now?'

'None at all,' Wood replied, with a small white lie. The fact that she was still holding his hand gave him the courage to continue. 'What you said with regard to McRae gives me hope that you would not be offended if I were to pay you more attention. Am I wrong in thinking that?'

'I've been waiting a long time for that to happen, Fernando,' she shyly owned up. Then she gave his hand a quick twist, causing him to give a sharp cry of pain. 'Forgive me for hurting you, but I did it deliberately as a test. Your hand won't be fit for gunplay for some time yet. Remember that.'

'I will. But it's coming on fine, thanks to you,' Wood smiled at her as he put a foot in a stirrup and swung up into the saddle. 'I'll see you this evening. Until all this is over, it would be best if you didn't say anything to McRae about the way in which you regard him.'

'I won't,' Heather promised.

A saddened Martha Tinkler looked around the crowded old barn that was the nearest thing Gray's Flat had to a town hall. She had just discovered that the formerly charming Durell had snatched her dream project for a town council from her. Clutching the now redundant script of the speech she had laboured long and hard to perfect, she was on the verge of tears.

On an improvised stage, Durell and Max Nelson sat with Juanita at Nelson's side, her stunning looks being used to boost her husband's celebrity status. Durell got to his feet to rob Miss Tinkler of what should rightly have been her glorious moment.

'Ladies and gentlemen,' he began in his educated manner of speaking. 'History is being made here tonight, and you are a part of it. This is the time when Gray's Flat comes of age. You will be asking yourselves, who is this man speaking to us about our town. It is true that I am a stranger, but a stranger who can see the potential that your town holds. I have served as a congressman, and my experience in government is why I have been asked to chair this meeting.'

This was an outright lie that made it impossible for Miss Tinkler to hold back her tears. Seeing her weeping, Sue Alton, the storekeeper's wife, and Martha's friend, moved closer to put a comforting arm round her.

Durell was speaking again, introducing the twelve candidates who, apart from Max Nelson, were unremarkable, uninspiring Gray's Flat residents. Sheriff Fernando Wood, who stood with Zec and Heather Cordell, Maury McRae, and Ernie Roderick, voiced his disappointment to them. 'Poor Martha Tinkler. This is a scheme hatched by Nelson and Durell to produce a council over which they will have full control.'

The elections began. Voting was by a show of hands, and Durell had supporters in the crowd to ensure that Max Nelson and five of the slightly less obvious inadequates were elected.

'Democracy has come to Gray's Flat,' he announced smugly. 'In the way that any group must have a leader, so must the embryonic Gray's Flat Town Council have a mayor. It will not harm the democratic process one iota for me to put forward Max Nelson as the man most capable of leading this small town into an era of mature and responsible prosperity.'

There was no objection. Nelson stood, speaking from the speech that Durell had written for him. Speaking of his plans for a railroad, he then introduced the subject of law and order.

'Every prosperous town inevitably attracts the lawless. What we need, right from this very moment is a lawman of our very own. I have already been given the approval of my council colleagues to carry out my first duty as mayor by appointing Mr Durell as Town Marshal.'

There was some muted applause as Nelson sat down and Durell stood up and spoke of what a proud moment it was for him. 'One major regret that I do have is that my duties must begin right now, and in a most distasteful way.' He turned to pick up a sheet of paper from the trestle. Studying it for some time, he then raised his head to address the crowd. 'What I'm holding here is a wanted poster picturing a renegade with a high price on his head.

'This dangerous outlaw has been living in the area for some time now. By concealing his identity, he tricked Mr Nelson into giving him work at the *Two Circles* ranch in Cottonwood Valley. Yesterday, when you were going about your business, this outlaw shot a *Two Circles* ranch hand dead in cold blood, a murder witnessed by both Mr Max Nelson and his son Reuben.

'You will ask, how did this wanted man come to dwell in our midst for so long? The man in question, whose name is McRae, is in this hall with you right now, and the reason why he has been free is standing beside him. That is the man paid to keep law and order, Sheriff Wood. I say to you, Sheriff Wood, if you do not take this man into custody at once, I will come looking for you at midnight. Then you will be facing me in a showdown.'

Restlessness in the crowd had Sheriff Wood and his group move out into the night, where Wood's name was called whisperingly from the shadows of an alleyway. Both the sheriff and McRae relaxed when Martha Tinkler came out of the darkness into the comparative light of the street. She invited all of them to stay at her house for the night.

'That's very kind of you, Miss Tinkler,' Sheriff Woods responded to the invitation. 'I do think it best that all of us stay in town for the night. May I express my sorrow that your good intentions in respect of forming a town council were so crudely abused.'

'Thank you, Sheriff,' Martha Tinkler said in a choked voice. 'Now, please, all of you come along and make yourself comfortable in my home. Mr Durell will not be coming back.'

'I'll need to see to the horses first,' McRae said. 'Is there a stables in Gray's Flat, Miss Tinkler?'

'There isn't, I'm afraid. But Mr Bugler, who runs a freight business, keeps his horses in a compound down that way. I'm sure that he won't mind your horses being in there for the night.'

'Thank you,' McRae said as he moved away.

Reaching the Cordells's buckboard, McRae unhitched the horse and led it with others to the enclosure Martha Tinkler had directed him to. Back out on the street, an approaching rider had him pull into the shadows and wait. The horse slowed and stopped exactly where McRae had hidden himself. In weak moonlight he recognized the rider's profile. It was Juanita Nelson.

'How did you know I was here?' he asked.

'It was easy,' she replied. 'We are soul mates, Maury. I

sensed your presence the way one twin is in some mysterious way in touch with the other twin.'

Stepping out to stand beside her horse, he said, 'I'm not aware of you in that way, Juanita.'

'I'm sure that deep inside you are. It's just that men aren't as sensitive as women. I've been looking for you, anyway. Max and Durell know that you and the sheriff are at Martha Tinkler's place. They plan to get rid of both you and Fernando Wood. At midnight, Durell is coming there to call Fernando out, then he is going to deal with you.'

'He'll be lucky to beat Wood to the draw.'

'Luck will play no part in it,' Juanita informed him. 'Just down the street from Martha's house there's an old wagon in a gap between Alton's store and the Ace of Diamonds saloon.'

'Which means?'

'Reuben will be in that wagon with a rifle. Lying in wait.'

Deeply indebted to her for this information, McRae expressed his thanks. 'I really appreciate your help, Juanita.'

She was a half silhouetted in the pale light of the night, but he was able to see the shoulders rise and fall in a shrug. 'Like I told you before, my pleasure comes from causing my husband problems. I suppose it's now a case of *hasta la vista*, Maury. Do you think it possible that we'll ever meet again, either in this world or the next?'

'I'm not so sure there is a next world, so I'll look forward to seeing you again in this one. Until then, Juanita, *vaya con Dios.*'

Her only response was a nod as she rode away into the night.

*

'Once I have dealt with Durell, Miss Tinkler, I promise you that I will have this ludicrous council disbanded, and give you every support in creating the town council you had planned.'

In the kitchen, Heather heard Fernando Wood consoling and reassuring a distraught Martha Tinider. The sound of the front door opening announced the arrival of McRae. She quietly closed the door to the dining room so their conversation would not be overheard.

The serious expression on his face had her ask, 'What's happening, Maury?'

He glanced at a long case clock standing in a corner. 'In half-an-hour's time, at midnight, Durell is coming for Sheriff Wood. I have to warn him that it won't be a fair fight. Reuben Nelson is lying in wait with a rifle.'

'We can't let Fernando go out there,' she whispered, her face ashen.

'He's a fast gun, Heather. My guess is that he'll have the edge on Durell, and he's too experienced to be caught by Reuben.'

'It's not that,' she said despairingly. Head bowed, she fell silent, then looked up at him. 'I'm betraying a confidence now, Maury, but I have no option. Fernando has a problem with his right wrist. He couldn't beat Zee to the draw right now.'

'Then I'll have to tell him that I'll take his place against Durell.'

She shook her head. 'He won't agree to that. He's a proud man, Maury.'

'You're right. Give me a moment.'

They both remained silent as McRae rolled a cigarette, lit up, and took a deep drag. As he exhaled smoke he began talking. 'This is what we'll do, Heather. You tell him

154

what I told you about Durell coming for him, and that Nelson's son is hiding nearby with a rifle. I'm going out to get Reuben now before Durell can get here. You tell Wood that. What you don't tell him is that after I have taken care of the Nelson boy, I will face Durell before he can call the sheriff out.'

He was making his way to the door when Heather reached out to catch hold of his hand. 'You are a good man, Maury McRae.'

'I'm not, and I never have been,' he told her, tenderly squeezing her hand, 'but when I come back I'm going to prove to you that I can be.'

Desperate to put him right, to say that what he was wishing for never could be, she had to accept that this wasn't the time to do so. So she said simply. 'Make sure that you do come back.'

The *Ace of Diamonds* was in darkness when McRae slipped quietly through a gap between the side wall of the building and a decrepit wagon. Moving carefully to the wagon's rear, he gripped the tailboard with both hands. Bracing himself, relying on the element of surprise, he bent his knees, pulled on the tailboard with his hands to spring up into the wagon.

In the dim light he could make out Reuben Nelson lying face down, cradling a rifle. Within a split second, McRae learned that Nelson's reflexes were perfect, and his movements were astonishingly swift for so big a man. As McRae landed on his hands and knees, Nelson spun round and swung his rifle by the barrel. The butt cracked hard against the side of McRae's head. Partially conscious, he was aware of the weight of the huge body on top of him, and Nelson's fingers around his throat, throttling him. Suffering from a lack of air, McRae tried in vain to twist his body out from under that of Nelson. Time was growing short. He would be fortunate if he had half a minute left before he blacked out.

Easing his right side up a little from the bed of the wagon, he slid a hand awkwardly in under himself. More easily than he expected, his hand located and grasped the handle of a knife in the sheath attached to his belt. Using the last vestiges of his strength, he pulled the knife from the sheath; let his body drop back on to the wagon bed, while at the same time swinging his arm upwards and inwards. Feeling the blade grating against bones, then finding a gap between ribs and thrusting deep into Nelson's chest, he felt the powerful fingers relax their strangling grip, while he distinctly heard the death rattle in the throat of Reuben Nelson.

Taking in great gulps of air that tortured his lungs, he rapidly regained enough physical power to roll the heavy dead body off him. Clambering out of the wagon, he leaned against it, breathing deeply to steady himself. Still not fully recovered, he became aware of the figure of a man walking slowly up the centre of the street towards him. It had to be Durell, and McRae, though far from ready for a confrontation, knew what he must do. Using a shoulder against the wagon to push himself upright, he walked out to the centre of the street.

Catching sight of him, Durell slowed his pace but kept on coming. Waiting for him, McRae felt a great exhilaration. He saw Durell as his past life that had to be wiped out. In the next few moments, fate would decide whether he would be starting anew with Heather Cordell by his side, or would lie dead in the dusty, dirty street of this godforsaken little town. The latter possibility didn't cause him any real sense of dread. It was preferable to a continuation of life on the run. There was probably little or no difference between his speed with a gun and that of Duren. But if he proved to be the superior gunfighter, then in Heather he really had something to live for. He was standing square on to Durell, waiting for the bounty hunter to make his first move, when a shout came from behind him.

'Stand aside, McRae.'

It was the voice of Fernando Wood, and the sound of it sent an icy jolt through McRae's body. Heather had been unable to stop the sheriff from coming out on the street to face what would most certainly be his death. Without turning, keeping a close watch on Durell, McRae said. 'That wouldn't be a good idea right now, Sheriff.'

'I said stand aside, McRae,' an adamant Wood commanded.

The situation was an impossible one for McRae. Should he refuse to move, it would be an insult to Fernando Wood. If he moved, then he would surely be signing the death warrant of a sheriff handicapped by a faulty gun hand. He had no choice. Walking backwards towards the wagon, he watched the gap between Durell and Wood gradually close.

'The prediction I made in Etheridge has come true, Wood,' Durell said in an amused tone. 'This is verily a meeting of gladiators. We stand before the greater Caesar in the sky, and though one of us is about to die, this night we both shall be exalted. I salute you.'

'Stop talking and start fighting, Durell,' Wood hissed.

Both men went for their guns, but a horrified McRae heard only one shot. He saw the sheriff spin as a bullet knocked him off balance, and then crumple in slow motion to the ground. A woman's scream pierced the night awesomely. Aware that it was Heather, he stepped forwards to face Durell once more.

With his gun back in its holster, the bounty hunter said sneeringly. 'Now it is your turn to die, McRae. There is no victory in this for me, only financial reward, for you will never be the man that Fernando Wood was.'

Durell went for his gun as he spoke his penultimate word. Having anticipated this, McRae drew and fired. He saw Durell hurtled backwards by the force of the bullet that hit him, and felt the air disturbed close to him as the bounty hunter's bullet went harmlessly past him. Turning, he hurried back to where the sheriff was lying, with a sobbing Heather kneeling beside him.

His step faltering for a moment as the scene brought home to him that though he had freed himself from the past, Heather was not going to be there for him in the future. It grieved him to see the sheriff's gun was still in its holster. Then he hurried on to kneel and turn Fernando Wood gently on to his back. He breathed a sigh of relief and told Heather, 'He'll be all right. The bullet caught him in the left shoulder.'

'Thank God,' she gasped through her tears, and as Zec and Ernie Roderick came out of Martha Tinkler's house, she said, 'Please help me carry him inside.'

The following Monday morning, an unshaven, dishevelled Max Nelson opened the door of the ranch house to find Calumet McClurg and Silas Rayburn standing there. Both showed shock at Nelson's unkempt appearance. Both expected him to move to one side and invite them in. But he stood squarely in the doorway.

'I take it that everything is in order, Nelson,' McClurg

said tersely.

In response, Nelson shook his head dumbly. Annoyed by this, Silas Rayburn coldly uttered a threat. 'You haven't achieved what you promised, have you? Make no mistake about it, Nelson. We will take you to court and hang you out to dry.'

Both men took a step backwards as rage erupted in Nelson, and he shouted at them. 'My son is dead, and my wife has left me. Do whatever you will. Sue me, you blasted vultures. Take me to court; crucify me if it suits you. I just don't give a damn about anything any more.'

Taking a step back, he slammed the door in their faces.

Heather stood beside Fernando Wood, whose left arm was in a sling; while beside them Zec had his arm round Elle Roderick as all four of them watched McRae ride away. It had been a harrowing time for all of them, particularly Heather, when they had said their goodbyes to the man who had saved each one of them from certain disaster. Though he had not shown it, Heather knew that parting from her had been an emotional experience for McRae.

As McRae and his horse were made smaller by distance as he rode into the foothills, she felt that, though thrilled to have at last established a close relationship with Fernando, Heather could not rid herself of a feeling that a part of her was leaving with McRae. She wondered if that meant she could never be truly happy in the future.

'There goes a lonely man,' Zec remarked sorrowfully, making Heather feel even sadder.

'I wouldn't think the poor guy has ever known anything but loneliness,' Fernando Wood philosophised, then suddenly exclaimed. 'What's happening out there?'

He was pointing to where a rider appeared on the crest

of a low hill just ahead of McRae. Watching with the others, Heather saw the rider come down the slope to join McRae and travel along at his side.

The sharp-eyed sheriff excitedly identified the rider. 'Well, well, don't that beat all! That's Juanita Nelson.'

'He wasn't lonely for long,' a relieved Heather said to herself rather than her companions.

Feeling easier, she linked her arm through Fernando's good arm and pulled herself close to him.